THE HOODED HAWK MYSTERY

The HARDY BOYS *Mystery Stories*
BY FRANKLIN W. DIXON

The angry hawk plummeted toward Joe!

Hardy Boys Mystery Stories

THE
HOODED
HAWK
MYSTERY

BY

FRANKLIN W. DIXON

NEW YORK
GROSSET & DUNLAP
PUBLISHERS

The author hereby acknowledges
his gratitude to Dr. John J. Craighead, falconer
and wildlife research scientist,
for his assistance in the preparation
of the falconry material
used in this story

CONTENTS

THE HOODED HAWK MYSTERY

"Looks as though Mr. Ghapur expects us to
become falconers," Frank declared.

CHAPTER I

Sender Unknown

"FRANK, come here!" Joe Hardy called excitedly to his brother from the front porch of their home.

It was early afternoon of a hot August day, but tall, dark-haired Frank, eighteen years old, ran down the stairs at top speed. He knew from the tone of Joe's voice that something unusual was happening.

When he reached the porch, Frank stopped short and stared in amazement. An expressman, who stood there, grinning, had just delivered a burlap-covered crate and a package. Joe, blond and a year younger than Frank, had already removed the burlap. In the crate was a fine, proud-looking hawk.

"What a beauty!" Frank remarked. "Is it for us?"

"It says 'Frank and Joe Hardy, Elm Street, Bayport,'" the expressman answered, holding out his receipt book for the boy's signature. As Frank wrote his name, the man added, "This is a peregrine falcon and you'd better take good care of the young lady. She's valued at five hundred dollars."

"Phew!" Joe whistled. "I'll say we'd better take care of her!"

"Who sent her?" Frank asked, then read, " 'Rahmud Ghapur, Washington, D.C.' Never heard of the man."

"Nor I," said Joe. "We'll ask Dad when he gets home."

As the expressman left, Frank opened the package. It contained several items which the boys decided were falconry equipment.

"Looks as though Mr. Ghapur expects us to become falconers," Frank declared. "But why?"

They searched for a note in the wrappings but found none. "We'll probably get a call or a letter of explanation," said Joe.

Frank agreed, adding, "In the meantime, let's learn something about falcons. Dad probably has some books on the subject in his study."

All this time the hawk, which was blackish blue with a black-barred creamy breast, had been sitting quietly in the crate, eying her new masters. Now she raised up, fluttered her wings, and cried *keer, keer,* as if she wanted action. The boys laughed as they carried the bird and its trappings through the hall and upstairs to Mr. Hardy's combination office and study.

Here the famous detective had several file cabinets of criminal cases and photographs of underworld characters. Frank and Joe, endowed with natural sleuthing ability, had had many opportunities to work with their father. Frank was serious and an honor student, while Joe was rather impulsive but always dependable. Though they had different temperaments, the boys made an excellent team.

Frank placed the crate on top of a bookcase in which Joe was already looking for books on falconry. Taking out two volumes, he handed one to Frank and began to flip the pages of his own. When he came to a series of pictures of the very articles that the expressman had brought, he said:

"Look, Frank, this is the leather hood. It's put over the hawk's head, so that she will sit quiet when she's being carried from one place to another. And one of these bells is fastened to each of her legs, in order that the owner can keep track of her movements."

Frank nodded and looked at an illustration in his book. "Here are those two leather straps. They're called *jesses*. One end of each jess is looped and tied around each of the hawk's legs. The free ends of the straps are fastened to a swivel, which consists of two rings connected by a bolt that allows each ring to turn separately. Both straps are tied to one of the rings and this long leather leash to the other ring. Pretty tricky, Joe, because in that way the leash never gets tangled or twisted with the jesses."

Joe's eyes darted toward the crate. "Think we dare try all these trappings on Miss Peregrine?"

Frank laughed. "Maybe. But first, let's find out some more about falcons."

Joe, reading on, remarked, "She's sure a fussy eater. Prefers pigeons to all other foods. But she can be brought back from a flight with any kind of meat or even this, if she's well trained." He picked up the lure, a short stick on the end of which was a thick bunch of feathers.

Frank, meanwhile, was studying the falconer's glove which had come in the package. "Joe," he said, "this glove must belong to someone from India or the Far East."

"How do you know?"

"My book said that in those countries falconers use right-handed gloves, while Europeans and Americans wear left-handed ones."

"Come to think of it," said Joe, "the name Rahmud Ghapur sounds Indian—or Far Eastern, anyhow."

Frank agreed. "But the whole thing's still a mystery. Well, let's put the hawk's gear on."

As Frank held the equipment ready, Joe carefully opened the crate door. Although not sure how to handle the falcon, he quickly grabbed both legs so that the bird could not use her talons. She struggled while Frank fastened the jesses, then tied the straps and leash to the swivel. All this time the boys kept a wary eye on the hawk, in case she should suddenly slash at them with her beak. But the bird made no such attempt.

"I guess the book was right when it said a falcon

seldom uses its beak for defense," Joe remarked.

After Joe attached the little bells to the hawk's legs, Frank pulled on the glove, grasped both jesses, and lifted the falcon to his wrist. She sat there proud and defiant—a truly noble bird.

"So far, so good, Frank," Joe said. "Now what?"

"We'll take the hawk outside and let her fly around a bit," his brother replied. "And let's get that old block perch Aunt Gertrude once used for her parrot. It's in the cellar."

"Good idea," replied Joe. "Miss Peregrine can sit on it in the fresh air when she's not flying. By the way, the book said that hawks should get plenty of exercise."

Frank nodded. "And while we're flying her, we can watch for the mailman," he said. "He's sure late today. Maybe there'll be a letter about the falcon."

Before they started downstairs, Joe suggested putting the hood on the hawk, but Frank said he wanted to show the bird to their Aunt Gertrude who was in the kitchen.

The boys and their strange pet got only as far as the first-floor hall when suddenly the falcon yanked free and made a beeline for the living room. Just then, the doorbell and the telephone rang. Frank sprang toward the front door and Joe headed for the phone.

At that instant the kitchen door at the end of the

hall opened and a tall, angular woman rushed forward. She was Mr. Hardy's spinster sister, who spent most of her time at his home.

"Aunt Gertrude, watch the hawk in the living room, will you?" Joe requested, picking up the receiver.

"Watch *what?*" his aunt exclaimed. But the bewildered woman received no further enlightenment. Joe was saying into the phone:

"Hello, Chet. Say, someone sent us a peregrine falcon."

"Great! What's that?" was the reply.

When Joe told him it was a hunting hawk, Chet said excitedly, "Bring it out to the farm, will you? I've never seen one."

"We will. I'll say good-by now because the bird's loose. See you later."

When Joe returned to the living room, Aunt Gertrude was standing stock-still, staring at the hawk, which was now alternately rising and diving from windows to furniture.

"Joe!" Miss Hardy finally managed to exclaim. "Get that beast out of here at once!"

Frank stepped to the doorway of the living room and reported to Joe that the mail had come, but there was no letter of explanation about the mysterious bird.

"What's going on here?" Aunt Gertrude demanded.

"We're flying a falcon," Joe replied, grinning.

"Obviously!" his aunt replied tartly. "But where did you get it?"

"Well, we don't know the person who sent her—" Frank began, and told her how the bird had arrived.

"Well, I know!" Aunt Gertrude exclaimed. "This Mr. Ghapur is probably some enemy of yours. One thing's certain—the bird is an ill omen and undoubtedly has poison on its claws!"

"Poison on its claws!" Frank cried.

"Oh, yes, I've read about such things being done for revenge!" Aunt Gertrude went on, her voice rising. "You and your father have made many enemies through the cases you've solved. You boys should have had more sense than to have accepted this hawk."

Before they had an opportunity to examine the hawk's talons for any poison, the bird suddenly lunged at Aunt Gertrude and grasped at her hands.

"Help! It's attacking me! Take it away!" she cried frantically.

Joe yelled, "It's that piece of meat you're holding, Auntie! She thinks it's a lure!"

Aunt Gertrude looked in embarrassment at the stew meat she had absent-mindedly brought from the kitchen. Frank snatched it from her hand and immediately the falcon returned to his glove. Then, after feeding the hawk the raw meat, he and Joe looked carefully at its talons but found no evidence of poison.

"Anyway, the falcon wouldn't live long if there

was poison on her claws," Frank told his aunt. "She'd be sure to harm herself with it."

"I suppose so," Miss Hardy admitted.

Joe put his arm around Aunt Gertrude. "The falcon was only doing what she has been taught to do. Pieces of raw meat are used as lures for training these birds. The falcon meant no harm."

"Well, maybe you're right," Aunt Gertrude conceded grudgingly. "But falconers don't train their birds in a living room! Take her out of here."

With this ultimatum, Aunt Gertrude turned on her heel and stalked back to the kitchen.

Joe looked at Frank, grinned, and told him of Chet's invitation. "Let's take Miss Peregrine out to the Morton farm," he said.

Chet Morton, a school chum of the Hardys, lived on a farm about a mile outside of Bayport. A chubby, good-natured boy, Chet had frequently shared in the Hardys' adventures.

Frank now took the hood from his pocket and attempted to put it over the head of the peregrine. The bird flew off his gloved hand, but the jesses and leash held her, and she soon stopped flapping and came up to a perching position on the glove.

"Boy, this is harder than I thought," said Frank.

Joe, recalling what he had read in the falconry book on how to "break" a falcon to the hood, said, "We ought to lay a small piece of meat inside the hood before putting it on her. Then she'll associate food with the hood and our troubles will be over."

Frank nodded. He said that the falcon is also fed a choice morsel of food after the hood is put on. Thus she connects a pleasant experience with hooding and does not struggle or fear the temporary blindness that the cover imposes.

After Joe had begged several scraps of raw meat from Aunt Gertrude, Frank managed to hood the hawk. He was awkward at it and resolved to practice until he could do it with a more deft touch.

As he carried the bird to the back yard, Joe ran to the cellar for the block perch. When Joe reappeared, Frank took the perch and said:

"I'll get the convertible and meet you in the driveway. You bring the hawk," he said.

"Okay," Joe agreed, taking the glove and bird.

He paused long enough to call good-by to Aunt Gertrude, then started toward the driveway.

"I'll wait here for—"

Joe's thought was suddenly interrupted. A figure, masked by a red-and-white bandanna and wearing a battered felt hat pulled low on his forehead, darted around a corner of the house and crashed into him!

The boy whirled and swung his free fist. But the short, heavy-set stranger dodged to one side and gave Joe a shove that sent him sprawling on the ground. At the same instant the man grabbed the leash, snatched the falcon from Joe's grip, and sped down the driveway.

Quickly Joe got to his feet. Yelling to Frank to follow, he dashed off in pursuit of the thief!

CHAPTER II

Peregrine's Prize

By the time Joe had reached the foot of the Hardy driveway, the thief was half a block down Elm Street. The man forced the hooded bird into a cloth sack as he ran. Then, seeing Joe in pursuit, he leaped a hedge and darted into a driveway between two houses.

As Joe reached it, a woman, leaning out a side window, gave a startled shriek. The masked man, evidently frightened, looked back to check Joe's progress. The side of his neck struck a clothesline, throwing him off balance, and Joe closed some of the gap between them.

"Drop that bird, you thief!" Joe shouted furiously.

The man staggered a few paces, then regained his balance. He jumped a low fence to the adjoining property and sped down its driveway, back to the street, still holding the bagged falcon!

Joe's shout and the woman's scream had attracted

the attention of a policeman on Elm Street. As the thief reached the sidewalk, he slammed into the portly figure of Patrolman Smuff, dropping the sack.

"Grab him!" Joe yelled to the officer.

But the masked man, recovering himself quickly, side-stepped Smuff. Forgetting the bird, he cut across the street and disappeared into the dense, flower-covered foliage behind a house. Just then, Frank swung the convertible alongside the curb. Joe picked up the sack and thrust it in beside his brother.

Patrolman Smuff had taken up the chase, and now Joe joined him. They searched the area thoroughly for two square blocks but were unable to find the fugitive or anyone who had seen him. As they retraced their steps to the convertible, Smuff asked:

"What's this all about, anyway?"

"That fellow tried to steal our bird."

"What kind of bird is it—a parrot?" the policeman inquired.

"No," Joe replied. "A peregrine falcon—a hawk."

"One of those hunting birds, eh? I didn't know they had 'em around this part of the country."

"This one was sent to us. It's valuable."

The patrolman grinned. "Valuable, eh? Did you notice anything special about that thief?" he asked.

"Well," Joe replied, "his face was masked. But this might help. When he grabbed the falcon, I got a good look at his hands. They were deeply tanned, so I guess he spends a lot of time outdoors. And he was wearing a carved ring with a ruby in it."

Patrolman Smuff jotted down this information. When they reached the convertible, he said, "Leave everything to me! I'll catch the criminal!" and hurried off.

Joe turned to Frank and both boys grinned. When had they ever left a mystery to anyone else to solve?

Inside the car, Frank gently lifted the falcon from the sack. She did not seem disturbed by her recent adventure. Apparently, since the hood had prevented the bird from seeing, she had not become frightened by the experience that otherwise would have terrified her.

"Since Miss Peregrine seems to feel okay," Frank said, "let's go on to Chet's as we planned."

With the falcon perched on Joe's wrist, the boys rode out of town. Twenty minutes later they were turning into the lane which led to the Morton farm. They saw Chet near a corner of the barn, making repairs on a door. The stout boy was alternately munching on an apple and hammering.

"Wow!" Joe grinned. "Chet's working!"

Although the Hardys needled their easygoing chum a great deal, they were close friends. Chet had been working with them ever since the days of their earliest mystery, *The Tower Treasure*. Just recently, in the boys' latest case, *The Yellow Feather Mystery*, his skill with machinery and the operation of his motor sled had helped rescue the Hardys from almost certain death in a sealed-up ice fort.

As Chet hurried over to see his friends, he called

cheerfully, "Hi, fellows! Did you bring the hawk?"

The brothers hopped out, with the falcon perched on Frank's wrist.

"Pretty nifty!" Chet remarked. "Let's see her without her hat." He reached out to remove it.

"Wait a minute," said Frank, "she's been through a rugged experience this afternoon," and told what had happened.

Chet's eyebrows lifted, then he grinned. "Sounds like the beginning of another mystery for you Hardys."

"And maybe you," said Joe.

"Oh, no," Chet answered quickly. "You aren't going to get me into the clutches of any masked man! "But," he added with a wink, "if you want to leave your hawk with me while you're off sleuthing—"

"Nothing doing," said Joe. "I have a hunch we'll need her."

"The hawk seems real tame," Chet remarked.

"She is," Joe replied, as his brother removed the hood from the falcon. Chet studied the notched beak, which Frank said was characteristic of all falcons, and the long, tapered wings.

"She's sure streamlined," Chet remarked.

"Yes, and she's a powerful flier," Frank remarked. "According to the book, she's very courageous—but gentle, too. Notice her dark eyes and the way she holds her head up. The ancient falconers called the peregrines noble and gentle birds. This breed was the prize of medieval kings."

Chet was visibly impressed. "Some bird, all right. How about a trial flight?"

At that moment his sister Iola appeared on the back porch of the farmhouse and called, "Hi, Hardys! How would you boys like some lemonade?"

Frank waved and said that he would have some later. But Joe immediately hurried toward the house. The slender, pretty girl, with dark hair and eyes, was his date on many occasions. Iola was fond of sports, and had proved herself to be a capable assistant when called upon by the Hardys to help in their sleuthing.

Meanwhile, as they walked toward an open field, Chet was asking Frank to let him fly the falcon.

"Better let me fly the hawk first," said Frank. "I'm not sure how successful I'll be, since all I've got to depend on is what I read in the falconry book."

By this time the two boys had reached the middle of the large field. Frank stopped, unfastened each jess from the swivel, and then, with a somewhat awkward movement of the glove, he threw the hawk into the air.

"I sure hope that she's well trained," Frank murmured as the bird took flight.

With long, powerful wing beats the falcon circled, rising higher and higher until she was merely a dot in the sky above them.

"Now what?" Chet asked.

"See this," said Frank, holding out the feathered lure.

"What on earth is that?" queried Chet.

Frank explained, "According to the book, the falconer waves this lure in the air and the well-trained falcon immediately drops earthward and strikes it."

"You mean she'll come back to that thing?" Chet said incredulously.

Frank nodded, watching the hawk intently.

"See how she keeps circling us!" he exclaimed. "That's called 'waiting on.' She'll maintain her pitch there until I call her back, either by waving the lure or flushing a bird."

Frank swung the lure several times, then let it drop to the ground. Immediately the falcon turned over and plummeted toward them at terrific speed.

"She's stooping!" yelled Frank. "Listen to the wind whistle through her feathers!"

The falcon came within a foot of striking the lure, then swung upward and mounted almost to her previous height in the sky.

"That was sensational!" breathed Chet, round-eyed.

The falcon made a wide circle and then headed off with deep, powerful wing beats.

"Hey! She's flying away!" Chet cried out.

"No," said Frank. "Look! She's after something!"

"It's a pigeon!" Chet gripped his friend's arm.

"I'll call the falcon to the lure," said Frank tersely.

But it was already too late. With unbelievable speed the falcon closed the distance and then streaked earthward, striking the pigeon in mid-air.

The boys could see a tuft of feathers fly and hear the sharp report of the impact. The pigeon dropped to the ground, and the falcon, after mounting from her stoop, dropped down again to claim her prize.

Both Frank and Chet ran toward the two birds, hoping to rescue the pigeon. Frank slowed to a walk as he neared the falcon, and then slowly, in order not to frighten her, reached for the jesses. Wings and tail spread, the bird looked defiantly at him but made no attempt to fly off. The boy secured the jesses and put on the leash.

"Too bad," said Frank, "but the pigeon's dead."

He stroked the hawk, and then slowly lifted pigeon and falcon with his gloved hand. As he did, he saw a small red capsule on one of the pigeon's legs.

"Gosh, it's a carrier pigeon!" exclaimed Chet.

Frank made no reply, concerned that the falcon had killed someone's prized bird. He asked Chet to twist the cap off the small container. Chet did so and shook it gingerly over the palm of his hand. To the boys' amazement, instead of a message, out fell two glittering red stones.

"That's strange," Frank remarked.

By this time, Joe, having witnessed the falcon's performance, had joined his brother and Chet. Now the trio bent over the stones in Chet's hands. Frank asked Joe to check the pigeon's other leg for an identification band.

"Nothing here, Frank," he reported.

Frank looked grim. "And maybe for a good reason. A carrier pigeon wouldn't be flying two ordinary pieces of red glass."

Chet and Joe agreed.

"I believe," said Frank as he rubbed his fingers over the stones and recognized an oily feel to them, "that these are rubies—valuable rubies!"

CHAPTER III

Smugglers

"RUBIES!" Chet exclaimed in amazement. Then he laughed. "You're fooling, Frank. In fact, I'll treat you both to a dinner if those stones are anything but colored glass."

"You're on!" Joe grinned.

"Let's get to a jeweler's!" Frank urged.

Wrapping the stones in a handkerchief, he put them into his jacket pocket. The boys buried the pigeon, then drove to the center of Bayport and parked close to Bickford's Jewelry Store. While Joe stayed with the falcon, Frank and Chet went into the shop. The owner, Arthur Bickford, knew the boys well. He looked up and smiled.

"Well, what brings you here?"

Frank opened the handkerchief and revealed the two red stones. "We found these," he said, "and we'd like you to tell us whether or not they're genuine."

Bickford studied the gems for a moment, ran them through his fingers, then picked up his eyepiece and set it in his eye. He peered at the stones one at a time, then whistled.

"You *found* these? They're very fine rubies," he announced. "They might well be worth a king's ransom."

"Gosh!" Chet exclaimed. "You mean it?"

"It's the truth." The jeweler took another look. "I've never seen more flawless rubies. Where'd you pick them up?"

Frank evaded the question but remarked, "If they're so valuable, we'd better turn them over to the police."

The two boys thanked the jeweler for his help and returned to the convertible. As Frank and Joe began to discuss their great find, Chet quickly reminded them that the rubies had been found on his farm.

"That's right," Joe admitted, "so it means you'll have to help solve the mystery."

Chet winced at the thought of the work involved, but said, "Sure, and then I'll get my share of the reward for the rubies."

"Which," Frank added, "will make it easy for you to treat us to dinner. Let's see. When shall we have dinner?"

"Okay, okay," Chet said with a grin. "Any time you say."

"Let's make it right after we turn these gems over to Chief Collig," Joe said. "Chet, will you stay here to mind the falcon?"

The Hardys crossed the street to police head-quarters, and five minutes later were closeted with Chief Ezra Collig.

"What mystery have you boys turned up now?" the officer asked with a smile.

Frank handed over the rubies and said, "Mr. Bickford tells us these are valuable stones. Have you had a report of any robbery involving gems like these?"

Chief Collig said he could not recall any, but would ask one of his detectives, and buzzed for him. When the officer appeared, his superior relayed Frank's inquiry.

"Nothing like that has been reported missing," the detective replied. "And we'd sure hear about such a theft from other departments."

The chief thanked him and the man withdrew. They talked about the stones and the carrier pigeon for some time but could come to no conclusion about the mystery.

The boys left the rubies with Collig for safekeeping. When they rejoined Chet, they decided to forego his dinner treat for the time being and return home, since it was time to feed the hawk. Chet suggested that they let him off at his father's real-estate office. Mr. Morton would drive him back to the farm.

When Frank and Joe reached home they found their mother setting the table for dinner. Mrs. Hardy was a small, slim woman with blond hair and sparkling blue eyes. She welcomed the boys in a sweet,

soft-spoken voice, and it was obvious from her tone
and expression that she adored her two sons.

"What a noble-looking bird!" she remarked, ad-
miring the hawk.

Aunt Gertrude appeared from the kitchen just
as Frank noticed there was a plate at his father's
place.

"Dad's home from Washington!" he cried out.

"He's in town all right," Aunt Gertrude replied,
adding with a frown, "And when he hears about that
vicious hawk you boys are carrying, he's not going
to like it."

"Perhaps he won't mind when we tell him about
the valuable rubies our bird got for us," Frank said,
grinning.

When the boys related the story, the women
gasped in amazement.

At Aunt Gertrude's insistence, Frank and Joe took
the falcon to the garage, where they set up the block
perch and put her on it, unhooded. They fed her
some parrot seed, set the burglar alarm, and locked
the door.

Fenton Hardy arrived a few minutes later. He
was a tall, dark, distinguished-looking man of forty-
five. His sons loved his keen sense of humor and admired his brilliant mind and thorough methods.
Mr. Hardy's preoccupied manner as the family sat
down to dinner could mean only one thing. He was
busy on an important case of his own. Sensing his
sons' curiosity, he said finally:

"I've been asked to help on an interesting problem which has the authorities baffled. Immigration officials have learned of the large-scale smuggling of aliens from India into the United States somewhere along the Atlantic seaboard. One suspected spot is Bayport."

"Bayport!" Frank repeated in astonishment, adding, "Any other clues?"

"None. But maybe you boys can find some," Mr. Hardy replied with a twinkle in his eye. "I'm working on another case right now that I'll have to finish before I can concentrate on this smuggling racket."

"In other words, Dad, you're asking Joe and me to start from scratch. No leads or anything?"

"You know I wouldn't do that, son," Fenton Hardy replied, smiling. "I have two possible leads.

"A few days ago, while I was in Washington, I called on an old friend of mine—an Indian importer. I talked with him about the illegal entry of aliens from his country and told him I was going to ask you boys to work on the case. He naturally frowns on anything that will reflect on his country's good reputation, and has offered to assist in every way he can."

"Did he give you any leads?" Frank asked.

"No, but I mentioned to him that there must be some means of communication between the smugglers and their confederates on shore. We eliminated radio or telegraph because they could be monitored. But I thought that secret messages, instructing the contact here to pick up the smuggled men, might be sent by carrier pigeons from the ships offshore to the racketeers' hide-out on land. Ghapur agreed with me."

"Ghapur!" Joe burst out. "Dad, is your Indian friend's name *Rahmud* Ghapur?"

"Why, yes, son," Mr. Hardy answered in surprise. "How did you know?"

The boys told their astonished father about the falcon from Ghapur, the attempted theft of the bird, and the ruby-bearing carrier pigeon which the peregrine had downed.

"That's very interesting," Mr. Hardy said. "A call to Ghapur will certainly throw some light on the matter. I'll try to reach him at once."

Fortunately, the importer was at home. The detective talked with him for some time, then returned to the table just as dessert was being served.

"Mr. Ghapur says he sent the falcon to aid you boys in bringing down pigeons you might be suspicious of. He sent you a letter of explanation. You say it didn't arrive?"

"No," Frank replied, adding thoughtfully, "The letter could have been intercepted by the smugglers if they suspected what the falcon was to be used for."

"True," Mr. Hardy declared. "And it could have been waylaid in Washington, or anywhere between there and Bayport. In Ghapur's letter he asked you boys to get in touch with a fellow countryman of his who lives here in Bayport. He's Ahmed, the rug dealer. You know him. He'll teach you how to handle the falcon properly."

This statement caused Aunt Gertrude to speak up sharply, deploring the fact that the boys were getting mixed up in such a cruel sport.

"Auntie," said Frank, "it's in the line of duty. And anyway, wild hawks eat ten times as many pigeons and other birds a year than we'd let a trained falcon like Miss Peregrine go after."

"Well, maybe so," his aunt conceded, "but that hawk may turn on you any minute, as she did on me."

Aunt Gertrude then gave her brother a colorful account of her adventure with the falcon. Mr. Hardy agreed that it was unfortunate she had had such a scare, but he was sure that it would not occur again.

"Humph!" Aunt Gertrude was unconvinced, and was about to continue her tirade when Mrs. Hardy arose and started clearing the table. Her husband and sons got up too and went to the garage to see the falcon. After examining her trappings, Mr. Hardy said with a smile:

"It will be rather unique to solve a mystery with a hooded hawk."

"Yes," agreed Frank. "Dad, do you think there might be a tie-in between the smugglers of aliens and the rubies?"

"Yes, I do," Mr. Hardy replied. "And I have a hunch we'll find that carrier pigeons are the link between our two mysteries."

They talked for a while longer, then Fenton Hardy concluded with, "Well, boys, it will have to be your job for the time being to solve these mysteries. I must get back on my other case. From time to time I'il be in touch with you, though."

"You're leaving?" Joe asked.

"Yes. I'm flying back to Washington. Will you drive me to the airport?"

"Certainly, Dad."

After the boys had said good-by to Mr. Hardy at the airport, Joe said to his brother, "Let's phone Ahmed. It's not too late, and I'd like to find out how to use the hawk correctly, so that we can get to work."

"Good idea," replied Frank. "We should know more about properly training and flying the bird. We were just lucky this afternoon."

He put through a call to the elderly rug merchant. After identifying himself, Frank told him about the message from Rahmud Ghapur.

Though surprised at the request, Ahmed gladly consented to teach the Hardys how to handle the falcon. He said that they must first obtain permission from the State Fish and Game Department to fly the hawk. It was agreed that the boys would do this the next morning, then the three would drive out to the country.

"The Morton farm's the place," Frank suggested.

At the Bayport office of the Fish and Game Department the next day, the clerk looked quizzical when the boys made their request. When they explained it was in connection with a case of their father's, he gave each of them special hunting permits.

With their falcon and its equipment, the brothers drove to Ahmed's place of business. The rug dealer was standing in the doorway, waiting for them. Ahmed was a man close to sixty years old, but straight as a spear and lithe in his movements. His eyes had sparkle and life to them that demanded attention. The movements of his long, sinewy fingers had an almost hypnotic quality.

When the elderly man was seated in the car, he immediately turned his attention to the hawk. Putting on the gauntlet, Ahmed wristed the bird. As he stroked it, he remarked:

"This hawk is well trained. As a fledgling she was probably lured into a net, then hooded, and carried constantly on the glove for days and nights until she lost her fear of man and became tame. This is called 'manning.'

"The trainer strokes her, talks gently to her, and feeds her. In this way, the falcon becomes completely dependent on her master and learns that he intends no harm. Gradually she is made hungry or 'keen' and thus learns to respond to the falconer. At first she jumps a short distance to the glove for food. Gradually the distance is increased until she is flying several hundred yards on a string. Finally she can be flown free."

"Then she's actually trained through her appetite?" Frank asked.

"Yes," Ahmed replied. "And a young bird's instincts are channeled so that she performs in a natural way for her trainer. She is never taught to do anything that she would not normally do in the wild."

"Will she bring her quarry back to her master?" asked Joe.

"No," Ahmed replied. "She goes to the ground with her kill, then the falconer hurries to his bird. The hawk does not come to him. However, if the bird misses her quarry, she will return to the lure to be fed."

"It's a complicated sport," Frank remarked. "And I can see why it requires lots of time and patience."

"Well, one thing we do know," Joe spoke up. "Pigeons are a hawk's favorite food." He grinned. "But we didn't have a squab in our refrigerator, so for breakfast I gave her raw oatmeal and parrot seed!"

Ahmed smiled. "You'll have to feed her starlings, sparrows, mice, and lean beef. It's obvious that she is used to people and normal sounds, since neither of these bother her."

When they arrived at the Morton farm, Iola informed them that Chet had gone to market with a load of sweet corn. She promised to tell Chet where they were as soon as he came in.

The visitors strolled to one of the large open fields and Ahmed began his instruction. He suggested that Frank undertake flying the hawk first. Compared to Ahmed's dexterity, the boy felt very clumsy in putting on and taking off the jesses and the hood. He also felt that due to his inexperience the hawk must be tiring from the procedure.

"Let's give the poor bird a rest," he suggested. "In the meantime, I'd like to learn more about the history of falconry."

Ahmed agreed, and holding the falcon, he walked around the field with the Hardys. As they strolled along, the rug dealer told them about the short-winged hawks that are flown from the fist at such quarry as game birds and rabbits.

"These birds," Ahmed said, "such as the goshawk, the sharp-shinned hawk, and the Cooper's hawk are the best ones for a beginner to practice on.

"In my country, and in your country too, the peregrine falcon is considered the prize bird and only experienced falconers capture and train them. It is an unwritten law that novice falconers start on the less noble birds and by experience earn the right to train the bird of kings and maharajahs."

"Someday we'll train our own birds," said Joe. "We're fortunate to start off with a trained one."

"Indeed you are," replied Ahmed.

As the three walked back across the field, the elderly Indian gave the boys additional pointers on the care of their falcon, advising them to keep the bird with them at all times, so that she would recognize them as her masters.

"Remember," he said, "to put water out for her bath, to keep her in the shade, and to place her perch where she can't get tangled up. Above all," he cautioned, "be kind and gentle to her and she will reciprocate. Always bear in mind that she puts great trust in you; don't fail her."

Frank and Joe were about to assure him that they would certainly do their best to take proper care of their falcon when they heard a loud yell.

"Hey, fellows!" It was Chet, standing at the edge of the field and waving at them. "Quick! I've got news!"

"Good or bad?" Joe shouted back, as he and Frank started running toward their friend.

"Don't know—but you'll find out at police headquarters!"

CHAPTER IV

A Suspicious Sailor

FRANK and Joe sprinted across the field to where Chet was waiting for them.

"What's this news from police headquarters?" Joe demanded excitedly.

"All I know," said the stout boy, "is the department called and said you should report there pronto. It's real urgent!"

The same thoughts flashed through the brothers' minds—was it news of the rubies or of Joe's masked assailant?

"Okay, we're on our way," said Joe, as Ahmed caught up to them, the falcon still poised on his wrist.

The trio hurried to the convertible and drove to Bayport. After leaving Ahmed at his shop, the boys went at once to police headquarters. Frank remained in the car with the falcon while Joe hurried inside.

To his surprise, Officer Smuff was waiting for him, a proud grin on his red face.

"You have some news for us?" Joe asked.

"News! I'll say! I've caught your hawk thief!"

"What!" Joe stared at the patrolman incredulously.

Smuff strutted to the door at the back of the room. "Here—look for yourself!"

Joe walked over, feeling chagrined that Smuff had made the capture before Frank and he had picked up even a single clue to the thief's identity. The patrolman led the boy into a small room.

"There's your man!" he announced, waving his hand toward a sun-tanned figure slouched on a bench. Around his neck was a red-and-white bandanna, and he wore a battered felt hat. Smuff said elatedly, "I caught this fellow lurking around your house."

Suddenly the prisoner jumped up. "Meester Joe, you-a come to save-a me?"

Smuff blinked at the boy. "You know this man?"

"He's our gardener, Smuff!" Joe exclaimed. "Nicolo, I'm sorry about this mistake."

"I go now? I no thief, I tell this policeman. He play bad joke on poor Nicolo."

The patrolman, red-faced, murmured an apology and released the gardener at once. Then he accompanied Joe outside. "Well, no luck this time."

"Never mind," Joe said with a grin. "And don't hesitate to call us if you need help," he teased.

Policeman Smuff eyed him suspiciously, trying to decide whether Joe was serious or merely joking. When Frank heard the story, he laughed heartily.

Since it was nearly lunchtime, the boys went directly home. As Joe carried the falcon toward the back door, Mrs. Hardy appeared and asked that, for Aunt Gertrude's sake, the falcon be kept out of the house.

"But Ahmed says it's best to keep the hawk with us at all times," Joe spoke up. "That's the way they get used to their masters."

Aunt Gertrude, overhearing, called from the kitchen, "I certainly don't want her to get used to *me*. One attack was enough."

Frank merely grinned and took the falcon to its perch in the garage, set the burglar alarm, and locked the door. When he sat down at the luncheon table, his aunt remarked:

"So you think you should keep that hawk with you all the time? Ridiculous! You wouldn't sleep with it, would you?" She chuckled. "And I'm sure you wouldn't take a shower bath with it!"

This remark brought a roar of laughter from the others, then the subject of falcons was dropped for the time being. As soon as the meal was over, Joe, with a mischievous expression on his face, headed for his father's study. A few minutes later he returned to the first floor, carrying a volume of the encyclopedia with him.

"I don't suppose it would do any real harm to take

the hawk into the shower with me, Auntie," he told Miss Hardy. "It says here, 'Most hawks, peregrines especially, require a bath. The end of a cask, sawed off to give a depth of six inches, makes a good bathtub. Peregrines which are used to "waiting on" require a bath at least twice a week.' "

"Waiting on? You certainly do have to wait on them!" Aunt Gertrude retorted.

Frank and Joe exchanged grins, then told their aunt what the term meant.

Frank read on from the book in Joe's hands. " 'If the bath is neglected, the falcon is inclined to soar when flown, and may even break away in search of water, and so be lost.' How about that, Aunt Gertrude?"

Miss Hardy cleared her throat with a loud *harrumph,* then replied, "That might be one way to get rid of that hawk!"

As Joe was about to protest, his mother gave him a warning look not to continue the discussion. She knew that if the hawk should become lost Aunt Gertrude would be one of the first in the family to go searching for her. So why argue about it?

During the afternoon the brothers made a cask tub for the falcon and let her bathe. Then they laid plans for beginning their work on the case Mr. Hardy had outlined for them.

"My guess is," said Frank, "that anyone smuggling immigrants into the country would probably do it after dark. What say we take the *Sleuth* out in the bay this evening and scout around for a few hours?"

"Good idea," Joe agreed. "But remember, Miss Peregrine has to go along."

About seven thirty the boys prepared to leave. They changed to old pants and sweaters, then hurried to the garage, where Joe put on the gauntlet and signaled for the hawk to come to his wrist. When the bird was in place, he hooded it, and Frank drove to their boathouse.

After climbing aboard the sleek motorboat, Joe attached the bird's leash to the jesses on her legs and set her on a short pole in the wheel cabin, which was intended for raincoats and jackets. The bird accepted the roost readily.

Moments later Frank had the motorboat under way. As the craft knifed smoothly through the water, the boys were pleased to see that the falcon remained quiet. Presently Joe asked:

"What kind of boat, if any, do you think we ought to look for out here?"

"I surmise that the smugglers come close to the twelve-mile limit in a large boat," his brother replied. "There they contact the shore and make arrangements to have the immigrants transported the rest of the way in a speedboat."

"Sounds logical," Joe agreed, his eyes constantly scanning the bay in every direction.

Feeling a drop of rain, Joe looked up at the sky. In the distance he spotted a pigeon flying toward land. Grabbing binoculars, he trained them on the bird. Frank, too, had seen the pigeon. Both boys wondered if it were a carrier.

"Suppose we let the hawk bring it down on the beach," Joe suggested, starting toward the falcon in the cabin.

"I wouldn't this time," Frank said quickly. "It might help us more to know where the bird is going, so we can locate the owner. Get the pigeon's direction, Joe."

He handed his brother a pocket compass. Joe balanced it on his hand, and compensating for the bobbing of the speedboat, studied the movements of the settling needle carefully.

Frank and Joe were well aware that carrier pigeons' actions are fairly predictable. When turned loose at their departure point, they fly straight up into the air, circle, pick up the beam to their home cote, and set off in a straight line.

By the speed and assurance with which the pigeon overhead was flying, the boys were convinced that it was making a beeline for home. When the bird was finally out of sight, Joe remarked:

"That was easy. The pigeon was heading straight southwest from here. The question is, How far inland is it going?"

"We have a starting point for our search, anyway," Frank commented. "Say, that pigeon at Chet's farm was headed in a southwest direction, too."

"Right. And now, with a possible clue to the smugglers' mainland hide-out, let's do a bit of aerial sleuthing."

"First thing tomorrow."

Presently Frank turned the wheel over to Joe. He was just about to leave the bay and head into the ocean when his brother said:

"We have company."

A deep-sea fishing cruiser was coming toward them from the open sea. Frank picked up the field glasses and read the name *Daisy K*. The Hardys were familiar with most of the fishing boats in the vicinity and recognized this one as a weather-beaten sports fishing craft used for charter trips. It was frequently tied up in Bayport. But they knew nothing about its owner.

"Think she's suspicious?" Joe asked.

"We can't overlook anything," his brother replied.

While the vessel was still some distance away, Frank studied it with the glasses. Turning to Joe, he said:

"Take a look at the sailor leaning over the rail on the starboard side."

As the *Daisy K* approached, Joe adjusted the glasses and peered at the heavy-set, dark-skinned man, who had piercing black eyes. Both of the man's hands were resting on the rail, and at first glance he appeared to be just a tired sailor relaxing after a long, wearing day's work.

"What do you think, Joe?"

"Same as you do."

For a reason they could not explain, the boys felt sure that this was the mysterious masked man who had tried to steal the falcon! But on neither of his hands was the telltale ruby ring. In a moment the *Daisy K* had passed the *Sleuth*.

"I don't suppose," said Joe, "that we ought to suspect every sun-tanned stranger who comes near us." He grinned. "That's Smuff's approach. I did have a funny feeling, though, that he was our man. Shall we follow him?"

"We haven't a shred of evidence against the fellow, Joe, and anyway, we know where to find him if we want him. I'd rather keep looking out here for clues to the smugglers."

"Okay."

It was choppy on the open sea, and as darkness settled, the wind grew strong.

"I guess we'd better go back," Frank proposed. "The waves are getting pretty high and I don't think our passenger Miss Peregrine likes it too well!"

The hawk was finding it hard to retain her perch and finally Frank took the bird on his wrist. Joe speeded up and made the bay just ahead of the advancing squall.

"Too bad we couldn't continue our sleuthing," Frank remarked. "But then, it would be impossible for us to get near another boat on a night like this."

Joe nodded, turning to glance at the storm clouds. "We're still going to get a taste of that squall before we can make the boathouse, Frank."

"I know, and it may be rough even here in the bay. We'd better put on our oilskins."

After they donned their slickers, the squall struck full force. Frank took the wheel, while Joe nestled the falcon under his oilskin.

In a fury of lashing wind and rain, the *Sleuth* pitched violently, and Frank fought to keep the boat on course. Then, as abruptly as it had started, the storm was over. The wind died and the rain slowed to a drizzle, then stopped.

"Whew!" Frank exclaimed. "These summer squalls! How did the lady take it?"

"Like a trouper," Joe assured him, stroking the falcon. "And not a feather wet!"

About half an hour later they nosed the *Sleuth* into the slip of their boathouse. Joe set the falcon back on her pole perch, and had just closed the door behind them when there was a low rumble in one corner of the boathouse. The next instant, a blinding flash was followed by a sharp explosion that rocked the building!

A sheet of flame roared up the walls and across the boathouse directly toward the *Sleuth!*

CHAPTER V

Date Line: Delhi

STUNNED, the Hardys at first could see no escape from the flash fire which had trapped them in their boat-house. But as the initial shock wore off, Frank cried out:

"Open the doors, Joe!"

The youth swung them up as Frank gunned the boat's motor. The *Sleuth* shot backward into open water a split second before the fire reached its prow.

"Whew!" said Joe. "Frank, that fire was set!"

His brother nodded as he docked nearby. Both boys jumped out and Joe fastened the hawk's leash to a rowboat painter. Then he followed Frank, on a dead run, back to their boathouse. Frank, meanwhile, had grabbed a fire extinguisher from the wall of the neighboring boathouse.

Behind them, the boys could hear the watchman shout, "What's wrong over there?"

"Fire!" Frank yelled.

One glance around the Hardy boathouse told the boys that a single extinguisher would do little good. Nevertheless, Frank played it around until it was empty. Joe said he would run to the nearest house and telephone the fire department.

Despite the danger, Frank decided to look for some clue to the fire's origin. Just inside the boathouse door, he noticed a small wad of newspaper lying on the floor. He picked it up and shoved it into his pocket.

At that moment Joe returned with another extinguisher and the watchman ran up with a hand line from a nearby hydrant. With their combined efforts, the blaze was soon extinguished. But the boathouse was badly damaged.

The brothers surveyed it with a feeling of sadness. The place held many pleasant memories. Both boys vowed they would find the person who had set the fire.

A few minutes later the Bayport engines turned into the water-front street. But when the chief discovered that things were under control, he sent his men back to the firehouse. He himself remained to talk with the boys and the watchman for a while.

"How did the fire start?" he asked.

"We have no idea," Joe replied, "except that there was an explosion."

After a quick inspection, the chief was sure that an arsonist was responsible, and the Hardys agreed, but could offer no real clue as to who this might be.

When the chief had driven away, and the watch-man had returned to his shack, Joe turned to Frank. "Who do *you* think set the fire?"

Suddenly a thought came to Frank. He pulled the wad of newspaper from his pocket. "This might tell us something," he ventured. "But it's too dark to read here."

The boys returned to their boat to get a flashlight. To their amazement, they saw that the printing was in a strange, oriental-looking script.

"I'll bet this paper was printed in India," Frank said, "and if so, it's my guess one of the smugglers may have set the fire."

"There's one man who can tell us if you're right," Joe reflected. "Looks like a translating job for Ahmed."

"Think he'll be up at this hour of the night?"

The brothers decided that it would be worth a try to find out. As they were about to leave, Joe suddenly halted and exclaimed, "Wait! I almost forgot our girl friend—the hawk."

While he went to retrieve the falcon, Frank made arrangements with the watchman to leave the *Sleuth* at another dock. Then they drove to the small bunga-low where Ahmed lived. The house was brightly lighted. They rang the bell, and the rug dealer, dressed in a flowing robe of his native country, ad-mitted the boys and their falcon into an attractive living room, furnished in oriental style.

"What brings you boys out at this hour of the

night?" Ahmed asked, rolling up a scroll he had evidently been studying.

Frank and Joe took turns supplying the man with the details of their exploits that night. Frowning in concern, Ahmed took the pieces of wadded newspaper carefully in his hands and spread them on a bronze table top. As he scanned the lines closely a smile crossed the Indian's face, and he beamed as he turned back to his callers.

"This paper contains good news. The date line is Delhi, India, two months past. It is part of a story which reports that Prince Dharmuk, the son of the Maharajah of Hatavab where I came from, is coming to the United States. The boy is eighteen years of age, and is to finish his education in this country. I know that he will gain knowledge and valuable experience here. Prince Tava, as he is called, is a handsome fellow indeed."

Ahmed glanced over the rest of the newspaper but found nothing in any of the other items that could be interpreted as a clue to the identity of the firebug.

Frank asked, "How many people in or around Bayport would be likely to read a newspaper from India?"

The rug merchant wrinkled his brow, then replied, "A dozen, perhaps. I have six men from Delhi working for me, and there must be an equal number employed on the fishing boats in the vicinity."

"Thank you very much, Ahmed," Frank said, rising. "This information may shed some light on our case."

The Hardys bade him good night, returned to their car, and headed for home.

They were up early the next morning. After breakfast Frank suggested that they make arrangements at once to have the boathouse repaired. He telephoned a builder, who agreed to start the work shortly. When he called the local airport, he found that they would have to postpone their aerial search for the smugglers' hide-out, since the helicopter pilot was busy for the rest of that day.

Later that morning, Frank and Joe had a conference with Chief Collig about the fire and left the wad of Delhi newspaper with him. The chief promised to look into the matter thoroughly.

"Joe," Frank said, as they left police headquarters, "if we're going to use our hawk to help us solve the ruby mystery, we'd better do some more practicing with her. We may be needing Miss Peregrine in our pigeon hunt."

"Right. Let's go out to Chet's after lunch."

The Hardys decided to walk and carry the bird, since this would give the falcon an opportunity to become accustomed to them. Frank hooded the bird, picked up the falconer's bag, and they started out.

The boys talked all the way, knowing that it was important for the falcon to come to recognize their voices and thus obey them more promptly. By now, she came readily to either boy's fist for food, as well as to the lure.

When they arrived at the Morton farm, the hired man informed them that Chet had gone to town but was expected back soon. Not wishing to waste time, they left a message for Chet to join them, and immediately set off for the isolated spot on the property where they would release the falcon. There, Joe unhooded the bird and removed the leash. He then directed her attention to several crows which were flying over a clump of trees nearby and threw her off.

Some sixth sense seemed to warn the other birds, however, for almost as soon as the falcon had left Joe's glove, they flew into a thicket. The hawk circled for a while, then climbed upward into the sky until she appeared no larger than a swallow.

"Maybe we're going to lose her," Joe said, worried.

"I don't believe so," Frank reassured him. "She's 'waiting on,' expecting us to flush more suitable quarry for her to strike."

"Well, we'll give her some," said Joe, taking the lure from a bag and waving it.

In the same small falconer's bag was a little fresh meat with which the falcon would be rewarded after she struck the lure. But the falcon would not come down.

Frank now swung the lure and both boys looked expectantly into the sky. The next instant, puzzled expressions crossed their faces. The falcon was nowhere in sight.

"Now she *is* gone!" Joe exclaimed, frowning.

Frank, however, felt sure that hawk had not left them for good. "She might have dropped on something when we weren't looking." He suggested that perhaps Chet had returned and could help them search for the hawk. "I'll run over to the house and see."

When he reached the Morton kitchen, Iola was there alone.

"No, Chet still hasn't returned," the girl said, when Frank told her of the hawk's disappearance and their need of Chet's help in hunting for her. "I was just coming to tell you that your father is home. He's been trying to reach you on the telephone about something important. It's in connection with your new case!"

CHAPTER VI

Indian Intrigue

SURPRISED to learn that his father was back so soon from Washington, Frank dashed to the Mortons' telephone and called his home.

"What's up, Dad?" he asked excitedly.

"Hello, Frank. I've just received a message from Mr. Ghapur. He's coming here from Washington with a friend of his from India who has a strange story to tell us."

"What is it?"

"The matter was too confidential to discuss over the telephone, Frank. The men will arrive tonight. I thought you boys would want to be on hand."

"We'll be there all right," Frank promised.

Then he told Mr. Hardy about the falcon not returning to the lure. The detective suggested that his sons keep swinging the lure where they had released the bird.

"She'll probably return when she's tired of flying," he added encouragingly.

Frank, however, sensed that his father felt the same concern as he—what would Mr. Ghapur think if the falcon were not retrieved?

"We'll do our best," Frank assured him. When he rejoined his brother, he continued to swing the lure. For what seemed like an eternity the Hardys strained their eyes for a glimpse of the falcon. They had just about given up hope when suddenly Joe gripped his brother's arm.

"She's coming back!" he cried. "Look high overhead!"

Elated, both boys watched a tiny speck hurtling toward them, growing larger by the second. With a swish of wind the hawk flashed by so fast that the boys could hardly follow her flight.

"She struck at the lure!" yelled Joe.

"Hold it on the ground," said Frank.

In a long, graceful swoop the falcon came back in and struck the lure with a smack. Joe held it firmly and the hawk came to rest. He offered her the raw meat and then quickly hooded her. Both boys heaved sighs of relief.

"Guess Miss Peregrine's had enough flying for today," Frank remarked, setting the bird on his wrist.

As they approached the Morton house, Chet pulled into the driveway and invited the boys inside. The three friends consumed half a gallon of ice cream while they discussed the strange mystery which the boys were trying to solve. Frank told Chet confidentially of the meeting to be held at their home that evening and of its highly secret nature.

"Maybe it's about our rubies," their stout friend suggested.

As suppertime approached, Chet drove the Hardys and their falcon home in his jalopy.

"Let me know what happens, fellows," he called, waving good-by.

Fenton Hardy was waiting for his sons when they arrived. He was delighted to see that the hawk had come back to them.

"Our callers will arrive about nine o'clock," he said.

Night had closed in at the Hardy home and they were waiting for the front-door bell to ring, when, to their surprise, a cautious knock sounded on the back door. The boys and their father hurried to the kitchen and Fenton Hardy opened the door. Two men were standing there.

"Mr. Ghapur!" the detective exclaimed.

"We thought we were being followed," the importer explained, stepping in, "but I believe we have shaken off our pursuers. Please pardon this strange way of entering your home."

Rahmud Ghapur was a dark-complexioned man, about fifty years old, with lines at his temples that indicated a normally jovial disposition. Right now, however, his expression was tempered by the seriousness of the situation. His companion, about ten years younger, was introduced as Mr. Delhi, a trusted emissary and cousin of the Maharajah of Hatavab.

Ghapur added that the nobleman from India had assumed the name Delhi because he wished to remain incognito while in the United States.

"And for easier pronunciation as well," Mr. Delhi added, smiling. "My real name is Bhagnav."

Mr. Hardy shook hands and introduced his sons. "We'll go up to my study," he said, "where we can be sure that our discussion will not be overheard by possible eavesdroppers at our doors or windows."

He led the way to the second floor. After everyone was seated, Frank offered to bring the falcon to Mr. Ghapur, but the man advised against it.

"If the bird were to see me," he said, "the fine progress you have made with her might be undone."

Ghapur now turned to his companion. "Please tell your story," he requested.

The maharajah's cousin hesitated for a moment, then asked the Hardys, "Had you heard that Prince Tava was on his way to the United States in order to complete his education?"

"We learned it accidentally last night from a newspaper clipping," Frank replied.

"The prince arrived in New York all right," Mr. Delhi went on. "Then he was kidnaped!"

"Kidnaped!" chorused the Hardys, and Joe added, "When?"

"About a month ago. Ransom was demanded in rubies. We received orders to leave the gems in a certain place in India. The orders were carried out and the rubies picked up. But the prince has not been released."

"You haven't heard anything since then?" Frank asked.

"Oh, yes. We have received a new ransom note which demands that more rubies be left at the designated spot. The note, like the first one, threatens the prince with death if payment is not made or if the story of his kidnaping is published."

Mr. Delhi paused and looked thoughtfully at the floor. "I—I am afraid Tava may not even now be alive," he said somberly. "But his father has not given up hope."

Rahmud Ghapur picked up the thread of the story. "The maharajah sent Mr. Delhi to this country to see if he could track down the kidnapers. Since I am a native of the same province, he came to me for help. I suggested that we get in touch with you, Mr. Hardy. Can you and your sons look into this matter for us?"

"We'll be glad to," Fenton Hardy assured them. "In fact, my boys may have picked up a clue already."

"Yes? How so?" both visitors asked in amazement.

The boys told them of the unbanded carrier pigeon brought down by the hawk.

"The pigeon carried two rubies. They may be part of the ransom," Frank remarked.

The visitors were astounded to hear this news and

agreed that the rubies might very well be part of the ransom. They thought, too, that the missing prince might be held at the place from which the pigeon had been released or at its home cote.

"More likely it's the latter," Mr. Hardy said. "We'll do our best to find the spot."

Mr. Ghapur leaned forward in his chair and said in a tense whisper, "Nothing must happen to the prince. He is like one of my own family. When he was just a small child, I was the guest of the maharajah for some hawk hunting and other sports." Turning to Mr. Delhi, he asked, "Do you remember the cheetah hunt?"

"I certainly do," Mr. Delhi recalled, "and the maharajah will never forget how you saved the prince's life, at peril of your own, when the boy was attacked by the cheetah."

"It was a great honor," Ghapur said quietly. He turned back to Fenton Hardy and concluded, "I guess we've finished our mission here, and successfully. Mr. Delhi will return with me to my home in Washington. Our enemies must not know where he is, so we will leave the way we came. We are deeply grateful to you all."

"We'll try to justify your gratitude," Fenton Hardy promised.

Mr. Delhi asked that they spare no expense in tracking down every possible clue.

When he and Rahmud Ghapur had left, as secretly as they had come, Mr. Hardy said to his sons, "I be·

lieve there's definitely a connection between the kidnapers of the prince, the rubies on the pigeon, and the smugglers of aliens from India. You boys made a start checking the coast line for clues. You might follow up on that, as well as trying to locate the carrier pigeon's cote while I'm away. I'm due back in Washington tomorrow."

"We'll keep after the water-front angle," Frank assured him. "And we're going to do some sleuthing from the air, too, in order to track down the pigeon's owner."

The family was up early the next morning so that Fenton Hardy could catch the first plane to Washington. While the boys were feeding and watering the falcon, their mother brought them two hundred dollars in cash and asked that they deposit it in the bank before two o'clock. They drove their father to the airport, then hunted up their friend George Simons, who owned a helicopter.

"No passengers ahead of us today, I hope," said Frank.

"You're the first. Climb in. What are you fellows chasing this time?" the pilot asked with a smile.

"Carrier pigeons and their home cotes," Frank told him. "We'll try to follow the direction a certain one took."

First they flew to the end of the bay and from there headed in the southwesterly direction which the two suspicious pigeons had followed. The pilot kept his helicopter moving along at a low speed while Frank scanned the land below, searching for likely spots.

Meanwhile, Joe was watching the horizon behind them for any slow-moving ship or small boat that might be plying between some steamer and the shore. He saw none but suddenly cried out:

"Here comes a pigeon northeast of us!"

Simons held the helicopter stationary until the bird had come alongside and moved ahead of his craft. Then he trailed it. For about eight miles the pilot kept the pigeon in sight without difficulty, while Frank plotted its course on a map he had brought. Then, suddenly, the bird made a dive for a sparse woods.

At once Simons stopped his forward flight and lowered the helicopter to get a better look. But something seemed to be wrong—the craft was losing altitude much too fast!

There was a screeching, scraping sound as branches and leaves lashed at the undercarriage of the helicopter. Desperately Simons fought to pull up his craft. At last he succeeded and they whirred up into the blue sky.

"Whew! That was close!" Joe exclaimed.

Simons grinned weakly and said, "I thought we were goners! Our motor nearly quit."

"Think we'd better go back to the airport?" Frank asked.

"Yes. No telling what this old windmill may do next."

On their homeward course, the boys again carefully scrutinized the area. There was no sign of a house or barn with a cote in evidence. The brothers were puzzled about the pigeon and its destination, but finally concluded that it must have been a wild bird and had just happened to take the southwesterly route.

At the airport, as the boys climbed into their convertible, Joe asked, "Where do we go from here?"

"We ought to go to the bank," his brother replied, starting the motor, "but let's scout around the water front first for the heavy-set, sun-tanned man wearing a ruby ring."

Joe nodded. "How about our looking for that suspicious sailor on the *Daisy K?* If he's the fellow, he may be wearing the ring now."

Parking their car a block from the shore line, the boys walked briskly to the dock area, where fishing boats, excursion steamers, deep-sea charter cruisers, and pleasure craft tied up. As the two headed for the *Daisy K,* Joe suddenly gripped Frank's arm and pointed toward an outdoor food stand.

"Look at the ring that fellow on the second stool is wearing," he whispered excitedly.

A stocky, dark-skinned sailor, who might well have been from India, sat there eating. As the man lifted a fork, Joe saw the sun sparkle on a ruby ring—the same unusual ring the falcon snatcher had been wearing!

Frank and Joe moved in on either side of him and

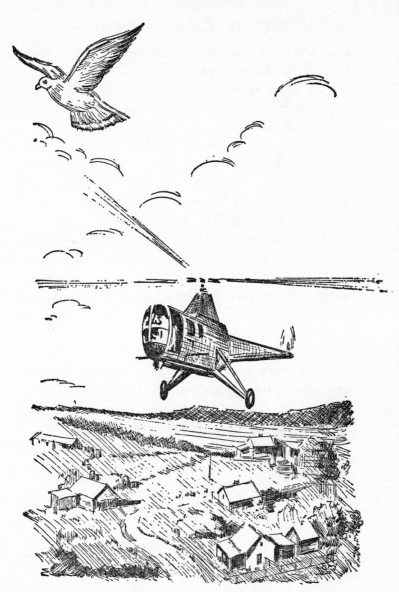

They trailed the suspicious pigeon.

took seats. At once Frank whispered to the sailor, "Just what did you want with our falcon?"

The man looked up, startled. "Falcon? You've mistaken me for someone else," he mumbled and backed off the stool.

Joe gripped him by the shoulder and retorted, "If you won't tell us, you can explain it to the police."

"The police? Say, what's going on? I don't know anything about a falcon. I swear it!" The sailor's voice grew loud and he shook off Joe's hand.

"Where did you get that ruby ring?" Frank broke in, stepping in front of the suspect.

This question brought a curious reaction. Apparently the man thought the boys intended to steal it, for he yelled, "Oh, no, you don't!" and plunged headlong at Frank, trying to shove past him.

Frank thrust a leg in front of the sailor, who tripped over it and fell. Instantly Joe came down on the sailor's back with a thud, pinning him to the ground.

"Now maybe we'll get an answer, Frank," he said.

CHAPTER VII

A Big Boner

AN INTERESTED group of bystanders had gathered around the Hardy boys and the sailor.

"All right, talk!" Frank ordered, dragging the man to his feet.

The heavy-set, dark-skinned sailor straightened up. Glaring at the brothers, he asked, "What do you want to know about my ruby ring?"

"Where did you get it?" Joe repeated.

"Well, I didn't steal it, if that's what you think," the man said sullenly. "I bought it from another sailor just last night. I got a good bargain, and figured it was worth the investment."

"What did this man look like?" Frank asked.

The sailor suddenly reddened. "Why—er—I don't know, but he looked something like me. Say, I can prove everything I told you!"

Turning, he yelled to the counterman to verify his story about the ring. To the Hardys' chagrin the counterman did so, saying he had seen the transaction. Frank and Joe looked sheepish.

"We're sure sorry," Frank apologized. "We—we made a mistake. We'd like to make up for it."

The sailor grinned. "Well, all right, you can pay my lunch check," he said. "I'm broke."

"Maybe we can do better than that," Joe spoke up. "Want to sell that ring?" he asked, recalling that Mr. Delhi had said to spare no expense in following up clues.

The sailor hesitated a moment, then removed the ring from his finger, named the price he had paid for it, and said he would sell it for a few dollars profit. Frank paid him for it, as well as the lunch check, out of his mother's two hundred dollars. The sailor saluted crisply and hurried away.

Shaking their heads ruefully, the Hardys resolved to be less hasty in jumping to conclusions. They immediately went to the bank to deposit Mrs. Hardy's few remaining dollars, then continued on toward the dock where the *Daisy K* tied up, but it was not in port.

"As long as we're here," said Joe, "we may as well make some inquiries about the crew."

They quizzed supply men and ships' captains. Finally one of the captains furrowed his brow, rubbed at the stubble on his chin, and declared:

"That sounds like a fellow named Ragu, first mate on the *Daisy K*. Heavy set. Piercing black eyes. Came from India. I've seen a ruby ring on him."

Frank and Joe could hardly believe their good fortune. That sailor they had seen leaning on the boat's rail must have been the original owner of the ring! The captain said it was Ragu's day off and he had just seen him in the Sea Foam Restaurant. The boys hurried there and spotted Ragu at a table in the far corner.

"Let's go," Joe said tersely.

He entered the restaurant and Frank followed. As the boys approached, Ragu glanced up and half rose from his chair, then slowly settled back.

"You're Ragu, aren't you?" Joe asked.

The man's face became impassive, but his eyes were gleaming. "What importance is that to you?"

"We'd like to know something about a ruby ring you've been wearing," Frank told him.

"I own no ruby ring," the sailor replied belligerently.

Frank brought out the ring he had bought and held it in the palm of his hand. "You don't own this now," he said evenly, "but you did own it. Where did you get this ring?"

Ragu's right hand whipped out, snatched the ring from Frank violently, and threw it across the room.

"You are evil boys!" he almost screamed.

Automatically Frank and Joe turned to recover the ring and Frank picked it up. When they whirled back at the sound of a clattering chair, Ragu was dashing out a side door.

The Hardys started after him, but suddenly Frank

stopped and said, "Joe, what say we let him go? I'm sure that Ragu's the fellow who took the falcon from you. If he doesn't think we're after him, and if he's connected with the senders of those rubies, maybe he'll lead us to them."

"Guess you're right, Frank."

The brothers walked back to their convertible. As they started to climb into it, a vivacious voice said:

"What a beautiful ring you're wearing, Frank. Is it a gift?"

Frank and Joe looked up into the smiling face of Callie Shaw, a close friend of Iola's. Blond, quick-witted, and carefree, she appealed particularly to Frank. Although interested, and frequently very helpful, in the boys' sleuthing, the pretty brown-eyed girl loved to tease the Hardys about their detective work.

"No, Callie," Frank replied with a smile. "It's a clue in a new case we've taken on."

Iola Morton had joined the group now and was talking to Joe. She said gaily, "Just the same, don't forget the picnic this afternoon. It's going to be a fish fry."

"Wouldn't miss it for all the mysteries in Bayport," Joe replied.

"All our friends will be there," Iola said. "Why not bring along that hawk of yours to the farm and give us a demonstration?"

"What say, Joe?" Frank asked.

"Count me in." Joe grinned. "And I guess our falcon can take in a picnic, too."

"It's a date," Callie said. "Be there about three. Games first and we'll eat at five."

The girls waved good-by and headed for a water-front fish shop.

"If we're going to show off Miss Peregrine," said Joe with a laugh, "we'd better go home and groom her."

When they reached home, the boys showed their mother the ring and told her how they had paid for it. She smiled understandingly and said, "It's all in a good cause and we'll be reimbursed. But if you find out the ruby isn't from the ransom, you will have bought a valuable ring cheap."

After lunch Frank put it in his father's safe. He and Joe fixed a bath for the falcon, then after changing their clothes and picking up bird, perch, bells, and lure, they set off for the Morton farm. They found a lively gathering of a dozen couples already playing spirited games of soft ball and badminton.

But the moment the falcon, hooded and seated on Frank's gloved wrist, was noticed, attention focused on the bird. Joe set the perch on the ground and said he would let her fly later. The hawk remained quiet as he and Frank joined in the games.

Finally Chet, who was wearing a loud dark-green shirt splotched with brown and white, said, "Show them what Miss Peregrine can do, fellows."

Frank looked around for a quarry. Suddenly a jay flew across the field at the edge of a woods. Frank yanked off the hood and flung the hawk in its direction. As the guests excitedly watched her fly toward the jay, a short-winged goshawk came rifling in from the woods and dived toward the jay.

"That's a trained bird!" Frank exclaimed. "See the *jungoli* about its neck."

"The what?" said Chet.

Frank explained that a jungoli is put around a goshawk's neck to keep it from snapping when the bird is launched horizontally from the wrist.

Instantly the two hawks started to fight over the jay. Joe started forward, calling excitedly to the falcon. Frank held him back, saying:

"It's too late now. They'll fight to the death."

But the falcon, suddenly alerted, shifted to avoid the vicious talons of the goshawk and then climbed up where she would have the advantage. While the hawks were maneuvering for position, the jay disappeared in the brush.

Frank and Joe now started to whistle and shout to Miss Peregrine, hoping to stop the fight. Suddenly the goshawk took flight and disappeared into the shelter of the woods. The falcon oriented herself, located the boys by the sound of their voices, and came down obediently to the feathered lure.

"Hey! You're pretty good!" Chet exclaimed admiringly, and the other young people applauded.

The Hardys smiled, relieved that their falcon was

safe, then looked inquiringly toward the woods into which the goshawk had vanished as mysteriously as she had come.

"Come on, Joe and Chet!" Frank urged. "Let's find that hawk's owner!"

Frank hooded the peregrine and placed her on her perch. Then the three boys hurried into the woods.

After a moment, Joe spotted a trail of recently trampled grass. Eagerly the trio followed it. They had gone only about a hundred yards when they were confronted by a large red-and-white sign:

DANGEROUS AREA! KEEP OUT!

The boys were puzzled, especially Chet, who was well acquainted with the woods. "Gosh, I never saw that warning before," he said. "What's going on here?"

The land looked undisturbed—no signs of digging, tree-felling, or other hazardous operations.

Frank noticed a similar sign some distance to their left, and Joe saw one to the right, both with the same words of warning. Nevertheless, they moved forward, but this time with caution. A hundred yards ahead was a string of similar signs.

Frank turned to Chet. "What could make this a dangerous area?" he asked.

"I don't know," his puzzled friend replied. "Old Mr. Smith who owns these woods used to encourage the public to come here."

"It's very strange," said Frank. "If any big project

were under way, everybody in Bayport would have heard about it."

"Let's split up and see if we can find out what's going on," Joe suggested.

He and Chet worked in a wide sweep on either side of the trail, while Frank followed the trampled path. The boys lost sight of each other as the foliage became more dense. But Frank could check the others' positions from the sounds of their passage through the tangled undergrowth. Soon even these were muffled, and the woods became a silent, twilight world.

Suddenly from Chet's direction came a cry for help.

"Chet's in trouble!" Frank yelled.

Instantly he and Joe were crashing through the underbrush to their friend's aid.

CHAPTER VIII

The Double Attack

FOR several anxious moments Frank and Joe could not locate Chet. But at last they came upon him, huddled in a clump of brush near a brook.

"He's unconscious!" gasped Joe.

They knelt beside Chet, then carefully brought their friend out of the thicket. As the boys placed him in a prone position, they noticed blood oozing from a wound on the back of his head.

"This proves he didn't have an accident," Frank said grimly. "Looks as if someone gave him a solid blow!"

Both boys glanced around cautiously to make sure none of them were in immediate danger, then gave Chet first aid. As Joe chafed the boy's wrists, Frank started for the brook to soak a handkerchief for Chet's brow.

He had gone only a few feet when he heard a slight rustling sound. Were they being watched? Looking around quickly, Frank spotted a movement in some bushes about fifty feet away. Without turning, he whispered:

"Joe, take care of Chet. I see someone. I'll be back as soon as I can."

Frank headed for the bushes, but almost at the same moment, someone went crashing through the underbrush. Frank increased his own pace, following the fugitive by the sounds of flight.

Several hundred yards farther on, Frank spotted the back of a tall, thin man for a fleeting second.

Then a moment later he heard a cry which sounded like *"Shabash!"* and wondered what it meant.

Frank put on a burst of speed which brought him closer to the man he was pursuing. They were both making considerable noise, now, as twigs and leaves crackled under their feet. For this reason, Frank was not immediately aware that footsteps were pounding behind him. When he heard them, Frank started to turn. Before he could see who it was, a sharp, heavy blow seemed to shatter his head. Knees buckling, Frank pitched forward on his face and blacked out!

Back at the clearing, Joe had listened to the sounds of the chase for a minute, confident that his brother Frank would be more than a match for any adversary. Then he went to the brook, soaked his handkerchief in the cool, clear water, and bathed Chet's wound. The boy's eyes flickered open and he looked up dazedly.

"What's happened? Where are we?" he asked.

"Take it easy," Joe advised him. "Someone knocked you out. But Frank's after him now."

"I remember. Someone rushed up behind me and I yelled for help. He conked me." Chet relaxed, closing his eyes for a while.

Joe sat down on a nearby log to wait for Frank's return. Glimpsing the sky through the trees, he could see that the afternoon was waning. It struck him that the picnickers probably were wondering about the boys' long absence. Should he try to get Chet back to the Morton farm and not wait for Frank? But Joe decided against this.

"Chet should take it easy," he thought.

As time passed and his brother still did not return, Joe grew worried. "Chet, I'd better look for Frank," he said finally. "Do you think you can make it back to the farm alone?"

"Guess so."

Joe helped him to his feet and the stout boy took a few steps, then stopped, admitting that he felt very dizzy.

"You better rest a while longer," Joe said.

He rummaged in the undergrowth and found a strong, heavy stick. Handing it to Chet, he said, "You ought to be able to defend yourself with this. I'm going to hunt for Frank."

"Okay. I'll wait here."

Joe moved off into the woods, trying to follow the general direction Frank had taken. Several times he gave the Hardys' secret whistle, which was a birdcall, and listened eagerly for his brother's response. But it never came.

Joe trudged on, following a trail of trampled grass he had picked up. As he reached a dense section, he heard someone moving just ahead of him. Joe stopped and gave the whistle again. There was no reply, but the rustling grew louder. He looked about for a weapon. He found a heavy stick similar to the one he had left with Chet, picked it up, and went forward.

As Joe crept around the bole of a large tree, he saw Frank staggering along. His brother's eyes were glazed and he obviously was trying to fight his way out of the woods on sheer nerve.

"Frank, you've been hurt!" Joe cried, gripping his brother around the shoulders and gently lowering him to the ground. As Frank looked up at him and tried to smile, Joe noticed that one of his brother's hands clutched a small pouch.

"Where did you get this?" Joe asked.

Frank blinked his eyes, looked down at the pouch as if seeing it for the first time, and muttered, "Don't know. Maybe—the fellow who attacked me—dropped it. Guess—I picked—it up." He sank back, exhausted.

Joe opened the small pouch and saw that it contained several reddish-brown nuts. He had never seen any like them and concluded they might furnish a good clue to the identity of the boys' assailant.

Right now, Joe faced a dilemma. Should he go for help and leave Frank and Chet? But he discarded the idea at once. Their enemy might return. He must get both boys away as soon as possible!

"Suppose you rest for a few minutes, Frank," he suggested. "Then we'll take off."

Frank closed his eyes but opened them ten minutes later, declaring he felt much better. Joe was seated beside him, gazing at the pouch.

"It's possible that we're close to the smugglers' hide-out, Frank," he remarked. "I'd say they might even own that goshawk, as well as carrier pigeons."

A few minutes later Frank said that he felt strong enough to start back. Joe helped him up, and the brothers moved off slowly toward the spot where Chet waited. Shadows were creeping among the trees, and the sun was low on the horizon. Because of the dusk and the condition of the two boys, further sleuthing was out of the question for the time being.

"But we'll pick up the trail first thing in the morning," Frank said with determination.

As they walked on, the boys discussed their experiences of the afternoon.

"Those warning signs weren't kidding," Frank said, rubbing his head gingerly. "This *is* a dangerous area."

"I have a hunch," Joe said, "that the pouch may be an important clue."

When they reached the spot where Joe had left Chet, the Hardys did not see him.

"I hope he wasn't hit over the head again," Frank said, worried.

Joe was concerned too, but he also recalled Chet's prodigious appetite and said, "Maybe Chet's stomach began to bother him more than his head, and he decided to go back to the picnic."

"No such thing," came a voice so close to them that the Hardys jumped.

The next instant, Chet's perspiring head and face emerged from his splotched dark-green shirt, which blended well with the leaves and twigs of the underbrush. The stout boy got up from his hiding place, grinning.

"Well, for Pete's sake!" Joe exclaimed. "You trying to play the hooded hawk?"

"I sure was! I need as much protection as your old bird," Chet replied, putting the shirt back on.

Frank and Joe roared with laughter.

"You needn't laugh!" Chet said seriously. "Those guys may still be around!"

CHAPTER IX

Hypnotic Music

As THE laughter subsided, Chet explained to Frank and Joe that he had felt too weak to fight anyone, even with the clublike stick Joe had given him. When he thought someone was coming, he had ducked into the bushes and put the shirt over his head as camouflage.

"But I guess it was my imagination," he said. "Haven't heard a thing since. Let's go!"

The boys made their way back to the trail and headed for the Morton farm. All the young guests had left except Callie. She and Iola were seated with Mr. and Mrs. Morton near the falcon's perch, keeping a close watch on the valuable bird.

At sight of Chet and Frank, the whole group ran forward. Mr. Morton asked, "What happened?"

"Got banged up a bit," Chet replied. "But there's nothing wrong with us that something to eat and a night's sleep won't cure."

"You bet," Frank spoke up, also trying to make light of their ordeal. "Anything left from the fish fry?"

"We've been saving some for you," Iola said. "Come and get it!"

While they were eating, the boys told the others of their strange experiences in the woods. Chet's father said that he would try to find out if Mr. Smith had posted the warning signs and why.

"Tomorrow we'll go back and investigate the place, anyway," Joe declared.

The Mortons and Callie begged the boys to be on their guard and they promised to do so. After breakfast the following day, a cold, dreary one for August, Frank declared he felt much better. He proposed that they take Ahmed along on their exploration.

"If we do come upon a group of Indians, his knowledge of the language and customs will come in mighty handy."

"You're right," Joe agreed. "I'll phone him while you get the car."

Ahmed, amazed to hear about the previous day's incident with the goshawk and the attacks on the boys, readily agreed to go. The boys asked Mrs. Hardy to keep an eye on the falcon, then set off in the convertible to pick up Ahmed at his bungalow. The rug dealer was hardly seated when he said tensely:

"If you have really found the hide-out of these despicable smugglers and can bring them to justice,

India will never be able to repay you for stopping this vicious traffic involving her countrymen."

Remembering the small pouch he had found in the woods, Frank pulled it out of his pocket and handed it to Ahmed. "I picked this up in the woods yesterday. Do you think it might be a clue?"

Ahmed's eyes narrowed as he scrutinized the bag and its contents. Then he said cryptically, "I believe we are indeed approaching the end of the search. These are betel nuts. Only lower-caste Indians chew them." Ahmed turned to Frank. "The person who attacked you and your friend may be one of the smuggled men or a servant to an Indian of wealth."

The Hardys looked at each other. The kidnaped prince, perhaps? He was indeed one of great wealth. They wondered whether or not to tell Ahmed the secret of Prince Tava's disappearance but decided not to do so unless it became necessary. "At least we should ask Mr. Delhi's permission first," they reflected.

A short time later Frank turned the car into the Morton lane and Chet joined them at the barn. Immediately the foursome set out for the woods on foot, taking a different route to the trampled trail they had followed the previous day. But just before they reached it, a new obstacle presented itself—a long, impenetrable wall of vines and branches.

"This will be tougher to get past than those danger signs we ran into yesterday," Frank remarked.

Ahmed paused and studied the barrier carefully.

"These vines and branches," he said, "are not growing here. They have been woven together by master craftsmen. Whoever had this constructed is indeed anxious to keep out strangers."

"I've never seen anything like it," remarked Frank. "Have you, Ahmed?"

"Yes, some of our hunters in India are clever vine craftsmen," he explained. "You have heard tales of the beaters who go out to stir up the tiger and the wild boar. They often use this weaving technique to make sure that the animals will not escape while the maharajah is moving in with his elephant, or the pig-sticker with his lance."

"Looks as though we should have brought along a machete to cut through here," Frank remarked.

Ahmed and the three boys picked up stout pieces of fallen tree limbs and started to beat their way through. Now and then they stopped to listen for sounds that might indicate trouble. But apparently they were alone in the woods.

Presently a disturbing thought came to Frank. "It looks," he said, "as though we may have frightened our attackers away from the woods permanently."

Joe nodded but made no comment. Finally the searchers broke through the thick mesh of vines. Joe spotted a fairly well-marked trail and went ahead, but suddenly darted back.

"Hold it! A snake! I almost stepped on him. Say, I've never seen one like this. Wonder if it's dangerous?"

Ahmed stepped forward. "Careful!" he ordered. "It's a *krait* and extremely poisonous."

The Hardys and Chet stared at the reptile in fascination. Between four and five feet long, it had smooth lustrous scales. The snake was dark brown in color and had pale crossbands, with occasional vivid yellow rings. Its head was small, and it was difficult to tell where head ended and body began.

"If the snake's poisonous, let's kill it," Chet suggested, looking for a stone.

"No, no," Ahmed said quickly. "It's a reptile of great value. We must trap the snake and present it to the Bayport Zoo."

"But how?" Chet queried.

Ahmed smiled. "You boys quickly construct a cage of twigs and vines," he said. "In the meantime, I'll try to charm the snake."

The man reached into the folds of his garments. To the boys' amazement, Ahmed drew out a reed pipe which he said he always carried with him.

"I usually play this for pleasure," he said. "Now it will be put to serious use."

Ahmed placed the pipe to his lips and began playing an eerie, hypnotic song. The snake reacted at once, although sluggishly at first. The boys were so intrigued by the rhythmic rising and falling notes that the music almost had them moving in time with the swaying motions of the krait.

But Frank and Joe quickly gathered twigs and branches, while Chet went for some of the vines which their enemies had used in the blockade. While they wove the materials into a sturdy, almost solid cage, and made a crude door, Ahmed kept the krait captivated.

When the cage was ready, Frank edged it slowly toward the krait. With the notes of his piping, Ahmed guided the reptile into the opening. Frank closed the door and carefully fastened it with a wooden peg and vine lashing. The three boys heaved sighs of relief and Ahmed put away his pipe.

"Good work, young men," he praised them.

"But the hardest part was yours," Chet said. "I think I'll try playing a reed."

"Hey! Who do you want to charm?" Joe asked, grinning. Then he became serious. "What shall we do with the snake while we're hunting for those smugglers?"

"Speaking of smugglers," said Chet, "do you think those guys put the snake here to poison us?"

"That is not impossible, of course," Ahmed replied. "More likely the krait escaped from a cage. Its owner would be too fearful of being bitten himself to let it loose."

The elderly man then told the boys that it was most unusual to find a krait in the United States. "The snake's natural habitat," he said, "is India."

The Hardys exchanged glances. More proof, perhaps, of the smugglers or Prince Tava being nearby!

Though doubly eager to renew their search, the boys first asked Ahmed to check the snake's cage. He did so, and said he felt sure that the poisonous reptile could not escape.

Frank set the cage to one side of the trail, where they would pick it up on the way back, and the group proceeded. They walked for some time, searching carefully for clues, but saw nothing suspicious. Presently the foliage began to thin out.

At the moment Frank was in the lead. He held up a hand for silence. Then, dropping to his knees, he crawled forward.

"There's a large hunting lodge up ahead," he whispered. "And there's smoke coming from the chimney."

Chet explained that Mr. Smith had built the lodge to entertain his friends during the hunting season, but that he never used it in the summer.

For several minutes Ahmed and the boys remained in hiding and observed the lodge, built of peeled logs. Then Frank said:

"It looks deserted, though someone must have built a fire recently. Let's see what we can discover. But be careful!"

Up ahead, the windows challenged them like suspicious eyes. Did the lodge conceal dangerous smugglers—or the kidnapers of a prince?

CHAPTER X

Scarlet Clues

THE searchers warily circled the hunting lodge, but they came upon no one, nor was there any sign of activity. Still cautious, however, Frank said in a whisper:

"Keep an eye on me, will you, while I get close enough to look through the windows?"

Frank hurried forward, zigzagging so that if anyone tried to attack him he would be an elusive target. At last he reached a corner of the low, wide veranda which ran around three sides of the building. Crossing to a large window, he looked into a handsomely furnished living room with a log fire burning. The room was unoccupied.

Frank moved stealthily from window to window. There were several rooms in the lodge, all well furnished. The bedrooms and kitchen showed evidence of a hasty exit of several people from the place. Dirty dishes were piled high in the sink, and bureau drawers were open.

Frank signaled to the others and they hurried forward. Moments later all were inside the lodge, looking for clues to the vanished occupants. At first glance they seemed to have removed everything.

Joe, who was more interested in where the occupants had gone than in the contents of the building, went through the kitchen and out to the back yard. At the edge of the woods he discovered a spring which flowed into a small creek. In the muddy earth around it were a number of footprints.

"Hey, come here!" he called. Ahmed, Frank, and Chet joined him. Joe said excitedly, "Here's evidence. Let's see where these tracks go."

"And look!" cried Frank, pointing in turn to several bright-red splotches on the ground.

"Looks like blood!" Joe exclaimed.

"Dried blood would be dark," Frank said. "That is brilliant red."

"And there are more red spots over here," called Chet. "Looks as if somebody was—spitting blood!"

"Your guess is close," said Ahmed. "This is a real clue. A betel-nut chewer has been here. A user of betel nut spits a bright-red fluid."

Their hopes raised by these latest discoveries, the searchers dashed into the woods, following the footprints Joe had discovered. When the trail of footprints ended, the boys spotted crushed leaves and broken twigs that marked the recent flight of several people.

Also, the conspicuous red splotches made by the

betel-nut user showed up here and there along the way. The fact that the inhabitants of the lodge had been in a hurry had made them careless, and therefore, that much easier to follow.

The foursome followed the trail to the edge of a rock-filled brook. There it was lost. Frank and Joe knelt at various points along the opposite bank of the stream, looking for some sign to indicate where the fleeing group had come out. But they found nothing and concluded that the fugitives had gone far downstream.

Convinced that there was no way of picking up the trail beyond the stream, Frank suggested that they all return to the lodge and try to find some clues to the occupants' identities.

"This time we'll make a really thorough search," Frank said.

Once inside the rambling log structure, each of the quartet took one of the bedrooms that opened off the living room. There were fingerprints visible everywhere but not one clear set.

Frank was going through the drawers of a bureau in one of the bedrooms when he chanced upon a small sealed box. The label, written in both English and what appeared to be Indian script, bore the words: *Krait Serum*.

"The people who lived here probably kept it around in case their krait got out of hand," he thought, as he took the box and a bottle of alcohol that lay beside the serum and hurried to show the others.

Ahmed took the items from Frank and carefully opened the box. Inside were a number of sealed capsules, each with its own syringe.

"M-maybe there are lots of kraits around," Chet said, wild-eyed. "We'd better get out of here pronto!"

The others were startled by the suggestion. Chet could be right!

"We'd better watch every step we take from now on," said Frank with concern.

Ahmed put the box of serum and the bottle of alcohol inside his voluminous robe, in case they had any further encounter with kraits. Then he left the boys to resume his examination. A moment later he called:

"In here, boys! Look what I've found."

The others ran to a bedroom which was furnished more luxuriously than the others. In his hand the elderly rug dealer was holding a dark-brown object the size of a robin's egg. It looked like a salt shaker, was delicately carved, and had a number of colored bands for decoration.

"What is it?" Frank asked, puzzled.

"A sandalwood scent box," Ahmed replied slowly. "It belongs in the luggage of an Indian prince!"

CHAPTER XI

Snake Trouble

"INDIAN prince?" Chet repeated Ahmed's words as he examined the box, sure that he could not have heard right.

In an undertone Joe said to Frank, "Prince Tava! This must have been his 'prison'!"

Frank nodded, then said, "I guess now we'd better tell the others."

Completely astounded, Ahmed and Chet listened to the story of the kidnaped prince and the Hardys' suspicion that he had been held here.

"I ought to put myself behind bars for not continuing the search yesterday," Joe berated himself.

Ahmed laid a hand on the boy's shoulder. "Do not blame yourself. Let your thoughts dwell rather on finding him," he advised.

"But where have they taken him?" Chet asked, adding, "I don't think I want to meet those kidnapers."

"Wherever the prince has been taken," said Frank,

"you can be sure the place won't be so easy to find as this one was. His captors will see to that and will make it dangerous for anyone trying to find him."

"Maybe now they'll kill the prince," Chet said dolefully.

A look of alarm crossed Ahmed's face, but he said quietly, "We must hope for happiness and good fortune for Prince Tava."

The boys felt slightly reprimanded by the remark and determined to follow the Indian's advice.

"What's next?" Chet asked, as he headed for the front veranda and relaxed in a comfortable rush-bottomed chair.

"I guess we'd better follow up the pigeon angle for further clues," Frank replied, as all of them sat down to rest before starting back through the forest. "I haven't seen any signs of cotes around here. I thought for a while that maybe pigeons were kept here, both as food for the goshawk and as carriers for the smugglers. But I guess that the pet goshawk had other food. Ahmed, do you think the bird could have belonged to the missing prince?"

"It is quite possible," the man replied. "However, I am puzzled as to why Prince Tava did not escape from his captors yesterday when he was evidently within sight of you boys."

Joe suggested that perhaps the prince was not being held against his will, but Ahmed scoffed at this thought. "More likely, guards watch over him every minute," the rug dealer said.

"It could be," said Frank, "that the prince has been given some wrong information. He believes it and is not trying to escape!"

"This is getting too deep for me." Chet sighed. "Let's go home. I'm hungry." He went back inside the lodge, helped himself to an unopened box of crackers from the fugitives' kitchen, and passed them around.

Both Frank and Joe felt that the mysterious house and grounds should not be left unguarded, so it was decided that as soon as the group reached Chet's home they would phone Mr. Hardy's operative, Sam Radley, to take on this job.

Radley and the boys worked closely together. He admired Frank and Joe's sleuthing abilities, and encouraged them in every way he could. Now and then, when things were going slowly on a case, he would needle them, but more often he called on them for assistance when his own sleuthing led him to a dead end. In order to be close to Mr. Hardy and ready for his orders, Radley lived in a hotel in Bayport.

Feeling somewhat rested, Ahmed and the three boys started back through the forest. As they neared the spot where they had left the snake, there was a good deal of bantering among the boys as to who would present the krait to the zoo. They were considering drawing straws for the honor of making the presentation when suddenly Joe spoke up.

"Wasn't it right here that we left the cage?"

The group came to a halt and studied the surrounding trees and shrubbery. All concluded that it was the spot, as Frank pointed to a number of broken stalks. "Those are the bushes we took the branches from to make the cage," he said. "And you can see where the vines were torn out of the shrubbery over there. It was here, all right."

"Golly," Chet broke in, "the cage is gone! Maybe that krait moved it by twisting and turning around inside and then broke out!" He looked around, wide-eyed.

"I think not," said Ahmed. "Someone has taken the snake. There are only two possible answers, both of them potentially dangerous. The owner may have come back and reclaimed his krait. That would mean that the kidnapers have not abandoned this area completely. Perhaps your Sam Radley will have more to do than you expected."

As the rug dealer paused, Chet asked, "And the other possibility?"

"Someone walking along this path saw the snake in the cage, and not knowing that the krait was poisonous, picked it up. He may have taken the snake along, or he may have freed it."

There was tense silence for a few moments, then Frank said, "If some uninformed person has the snake, we'd better find it—fast!"

They knew that this might be difficult. No one could know whether the cage with the snake in it had been found a few minutes after the Hardys had left it alongside the trail, or whether it had been carried off only a short time before their return.

Fortunately, there was a clearly marked trail leading away from the spot. The foursome hurried along it, peering ahead for anyone carrying the cage. Presently they came to a spot where a little rill moved across the trail, leaving a damp spot. In this moist dirt was a heel mark, which Chet spotted first.

"Someone's not far ahead!" he cried. "The water hasn't filled up this heel mark yet."

"We must be careful," Frank warned. "If it's the original owner we may be in for trouble. He may even try to use the snake on us."

"True," said Ahmed. "And if it's anyone not aware of the danger of the snake, he may become frightened and run off with it."

Realizing the seriousness of the situation, the searchers continued quietly but with speed.

Suddenly Joe cried, "There they are! A couple of kids!"

Less than a hundred yards ahead of them, two boys who looked about ten and twelve years of age were walking briskly in single file. On his right shoulder, each boy held one end of a long stick from which, midway between the boys, swung the krait's cage. The Hardys and their friends sighed in relief.

"Hey, boys!" Frank called.

The two lads halted and turned. When they saw

the three youths and the Indian following them, they became confused. One of them asked:

"What do you want?"

Joe, moving forward at a slow trot, said, "That cage you're carrying—set it down and stand away from it. There's a poisonous snake inside."

"Poisonous snake?" the older boy in the rear repeated. With a startled cry, he jumped back, pulling the stick from his companion's grasp. As the forward end hit the ground, the cage slid down the stick, striking hard against the ankles of the other boy. Thrown off balance, he toppled backward, smashing one corner of the cage.

"Roll away! Roll away!" Frank yelled.

Panic-stricken, the boy tried to comply, but part of his jacket had caught on the cage. A moment later he screamed.

"The snake bit me!" yelled the boy.

CHAPTER XII

A Strange Lead

THE krait slithered off as the Hardys and their friends ran to help the stricken lad, who was clutching his ankle. Quickly Frank drew the boy away from the cage, stripped off his sock, and grimly noted the tiny twin punctures just above the ankle.

"I'll use the serum," Ahmed said. "Frank, give him the standard first-aid treatment."

Unscrewing the bottle of alcohol, Frank quickly sterilized his pocketknife blade and swabbed the area around the wound. Then he made a cross cut over each fang mark, forcing them to bleed freely. Next, he put a tourniquet just above the knee to prevent the poison from circulating through the blood stream. The ten-year-old bravely gritted his teeth.

Meanwhile, Ahmed had taken out one of the capsules and prepared the syringe. He located a proper vein and administered serum to the boy.

"He's going through shock," Ahmed said. "We must keep him quiet and warm."

At once the Hardys wrapped the boy in their sports jackets.

Ahmed had arisen, saying, "I must get the snake before it bites someone else," and had pulled out the reed.

He piped softly, hoping the krait had not gone far. Presently they saw the snake rear its head from behind a stone and soon Ahmed had charmed it back into the cage which Joe had repaired.

Now Ahmed turned his attention back to the boy who had been bitten. He observed him for a few minutes and said that he expected complete success from their efforts. The others, sharing his confidence, settled down to wait until the boy could be moved.

Chet, meanwhile, had tried to comfort the older boy who had been numb with fright.

"What made you decide to pick up the snake's cage?" Chet asked.

"We saw it there beside the trail and decided it had been left by one of the zoo collectors," the lad explained. "Fred and I are working for points in our Nature Club and we thought we might talk to the zoo men and learn something that would help us. So we waited a while. Then it got pretty late and we had to be home for lunch, so we decided to take it to the zoo."

"So he's Fred," Joe said, pointing to the stricken boy. "What's your name?"

"Gene, er—Eugene Moran. We're brothers. Are you sure Fred's going to be all right?" Gene asked.

"Yes, son," Ahmed assured him. "The swelling is going down and he's breathing easier."

The frightened boy looked at his brother, who tried to smile. The Indian put a comforting arm about Gene's shoulder and said, "If you came upon a snake captured by zoo employees, it would be in a sturdy collection box, and not in a handmade cage built of branches and vines."

Gene's eyes opened in amazement. "We didn't think of that."

After putting the boy at ease, Frank remarked, "If you fellows live close by and hike in these woods often, you probably know the people who live at the hunting lodge. Tell us something about them."

Gene replied promptly, "Oh, this is the first time my brother and I have ever been in these woods."

"Did you see anyone else in the woods today besides us?" Joe asked.

"Yes, a whole bunch of dark-skinned people who looked something like Mr. Ahmed."

"Where?" the Hardys asked in unison.

Gene pointed in a southwesterly direction. "They seemed to be in a big hurry. Say, one of them, a fellow about your age, Frank, had a pet bird on his right wrist. It had something like a cap pulled over its head."

The listeners exchanged excited glances. Could the bird have been the goshawk and its owner Prince Tava?

Joe told the Moran boys that he and his friends

were looking for such a group of people and asked, "Were they wearing foreign clothing?"

"Oh, no," Gene replied positively. "They had on regular American suits."

"Did they have a leader?"

Gene thought this over a moment. "Well, I guess you'd call the lightest one the leader. He was tall and cruel-looking. Wore a cap something like a ship's captain, and a dark-blue coat. While they were running away, one of the other men called out to him."

"What did he say?" Frank persisted.

"It sounded something like 'Cap, got the stones?' "

Frank asked several more questions, but neither Gene nor his brother could give any further information. Presently Fred said he felt able to travel.

"All right," said Frank, "but you must remain quiet. We'll carry you to the Morton house and phone your parents."

Frank and Chet made a chair carry to transport Fred and they all started off. Joe and Ahmed carried the snake cage.

As soon as they arrived at the farmhouse, Mrs. Morton put the injured boy on a couch in the living room while Iola brought him a cup of bouillon. Gene phoned his father who agreed to come right over and take the boys home.

Frank then called Sam Radley, related the happenings in the woods, and described the location of the hunting lodge. Mr. Hardy's operative assured him that he would start guarding the place at once.

"But I doubt if those people will return," he said.

Iola Morton, feeling she could do nothing further for Fred Moran, had gone to the kitchen to prepare lunch. Joe followed her and she insisted that the Hardys and Ahmed stay to eat.

"We don't need a second invitation," Joe said.

A short time later Mr. Moran arrived. When Frank explained the treatment which had been administered to his son, the man thanked everyone for his kindness.

After Mr. Moran left, the Mortons and their visitors sat down to lunch. When they finished, Ahmed declared that he thought the krait should be taken to the zoo as quickly as possible.

Frank brought the convertible to the front door and the krait's cage was lifted into the trunk of the car.

The drive to the zoo was completed without further incident and the trio went in to talk to the curator of reptiles. The man accepted the krait gladly and said that the serum would be a welcome safeguard.

The Hardys drove Ahmed home. When they thanked the rug dealer for his help, he bowed politely at his doorway and replied:

"It is you who are helping my prince and my people. I shall be forever grateful to you."

Frank and Joe waved a farewell, and the convertible moved away. As Frank turned into the Hardy driveway, Joe looked at him with a grin and said,

"Brother, I'm tired and hot. A shower will feel good!"

"That goes for me, too," Frank admitted. "About the liveliest thing I'm going to do the rest of today is make up a list of pigeon fanciers nearby and try to find out if one of them has lost any carrier pigeons recently."

Before locking the garage, they stopped to talk to the falcon which was bobbing back and forth on her perch as though in welcome. Joe brushed his fingers along the bird's back between the shoulders and on the feathers of her wings.

"We sure deserted you today," he remarked.

After they had showered and put on clean clothes, Frank and Joe went to their father's study and started to check the classified telephone directory for pet shops.

"The owners ought to know something about pigeon fanciers," Joe declared, and Frank nodded in agreement.

The younger boy picked up a pencil and jotted down the numbers of all pet shops in the county. They made a series of telephone calls which netted no information. Not discouraged, the boys kept on. There were only three left on the list when Frank and Joe heard a noisy car coming down Elm Street.

"Sounds like Chet's jalopy," Joe said, getting up to look out a window. He laughed. "It is! And from the looks of the steam coming out of the radiator, he sure is in a hurry. Wonder what's up."

Usually the stout boy nursed along his prized possession as though it were made of solid gold.

Chet hurried inside the house and up the stairs so fast that he was out of breath for several moments and could not say a word. When he did begin talking, he could hardly speak above a whisper. Finally he extended his hand in which lay a capsule, similar to the one containing the rubies.

"Where did you get this?" Frank asked quickly.

Chet finally calmed down enough to speak and said, "I was standing outside the barn when I heard a plane heading for the airport. About the same time I spotted a pigeon overhead, too. Suddenly it looked as though the pigeon tried to pass beneath the plane. I guess they brushed together. A shower of feathers came down, then the bird circled and plummeted right into the middle of a field!

"And you should have seen that plane zoom," Chet went on. "I'll bet it gave the pilot a few bad moments. You know if that bird had smacked into the prop it would have meant real trouble. Why, I read in the newspaper just the other day about an accident like that—"

"But what about the pigeon?" Joe interrupted impatiently. "Was it dead?"

"No," Chet replied, "but badly shaken up. I put it in a cage and removed this capsule from its leg. Wait till you see what's in it!"

CHAPTER XIII

A Harsh Skipper

ALTHOUGH Chet had opened the capsule when he had removed it from the pigeon, he would not reveal the contents to the Hardys. Instead, he waited as Frank removed the cap.

Inside was a tightly rolled bit of paper which he released with his fingernail. He smoothed out the note on his father's desk and held it down at each end with paperweights. A message, printed in block letters, read:

CAUGHT L ABOUT TO SQUEAL.
HOLDING HERE.
NO DELIVERIES UNTIL REPLACEMENT
ARRIVES.

There was no signature.

Frank straightened up and slapped Chet on the back. "Good work, pal. This may help to speed up our case."

As Chet beamed, Frank turned to Joe. "I guess

we'd better forget those pigeon fanciers for the time being and concentrate on this new clue."

"You bet!"

They decided first to find out if the paper on which the cryptic message was written held any further clues. Holding it to the light, Frank studied the watermark. It looked like a fouled anchor insigne with several other figures that might have been porpoises or sea horses.

"Look at this, fellows," he said. "The next step is to contact various paper manufacturers to see if we can trace the origin of the paper."

From a list in Mr. Hardy's files, they selected the best-known ones first and sent night letters to the manufacturers, describing the insigne and asking if it belonged to a special customer.

"Now all we can do is wait," Frank said.

No report came in from the paper mills during the following morning. At lunchtime Joe said, "While we're waiting, let's check up on that man Gene Moran told us about yesterday—the one who might be a ship's captain."

"Okay. What say we try the Bayport water front again. Maybe the owner of that restaurant where we met Ragu can give us a clue."

The Hardys drove to the docks and headed for the eating place. When they questioned the proprietor about a tall, cruel-looking sea captain, he grinned and looked toward two men who were busily eating steaks at a table in a far corner of the room.

"How about those two?" he asked.

One of them was bearded and had a scar alongside his right eye. His companion wore a ferocious scowl on his unshaven face.

Frank studied the pair, then, approaching them, remarked:

"Pardon me. We're looking for a ship's captain who was out near the hunting lodge in Smith's woods yesterday. Was either of you there?"

The bearded man looked Frank over coolly, then asked, "What makes you think a seagoin' man would be messin' around in the woods? I was out on my ship all day yesterday. And a wasted day it was, too!"

Unseen by Frank and Joe, the restaurant owner had come up behind them. Wiping his hands on his apron, he said:

"These boys are looking for a tall, cruel-looking captain, men. Either one of you like to take the job?"

"What's it for?" asked the second captain. Then laughing loudly, he said, "A high school play? Long John Silver or something. I'll go home and get my wooden leg. Ho-ho!"

All three of the men roared with laughter. Frank and Joe reddened.

"I'm sorry we wasted your time," Frank said.

As the Hardys headed for the door, they overheard one of the sea captains remark, "Luigi, who are those two whippersnappers?"

To the boys' amazement, the restaurant man replied, "The Hardy boys. Their father is a big-time detective."

"Detective, eh? Zounds, Zeke, you and I will have to watch our step!"

Raucous laughter followed as the boys walked out of the restaurant. They visited other places along the water front but saw no one they thought was a likely suspect.

Finally the boys paused to rest near a small fishing craft. A jovial-looking man was seated in a rocking chair on the upper deck. Grinning, he called down:

"Are you the lads who are huntin' for a cruel-lookin' skipper?"

Frank and Joe admitted that they were. "How did you hear about it?" Frank asked.

"The joke's all up and down the water front by now," the man told them. "Just the same, maybe I can help you. If I were lookin' for a fellow of that stripe, I'd check with Captain Flont of the *Daisy K.* He looks like old Captain Kidd himself!"

The *Daisy K* again, the Hardys thought excitedly!

"Was Captain Flont's boat out at sea yesterday?" Joe asked.

"No, she wasn't," replied the man. "She was tied to her bollards all day long. I can swear to that, for I was a mite lazy myself yesterday and didn't leave port."

"Was the captain aboard the *Daisy K?*" Joe asked.

"Not until late in the evening."

The Hardys thanked the man and walked along

the pier to the anchorage of the *Daisy K*. As they drew closer, they could see signs of activity aboard the fishing craft. Captain Flont was poring over some charts in the deckhouse. Ragu stood lounging in the sun on the rear deck.

Frank and Joe halted at the gangway, and with nautical courtesy, Frank called, "Ahoy, the *Daisy K*. May we come aboard?"

Captain Flont, cruel-looking and harsh, leaned out the window and said sourly, "What do you expect? A full-dress review and a bos'n with a pipe? If you've got business with us, come aboard but make it snappy!"

As Frank and Joe stepped on the deck, Ragu looked up with an insolent stare. Joe peered at him intently in return, but the mate did not flinch.

As Captain Flont came to the rear door of the deckhouse to meet the Hardys, Frank decided that the best way to obtain the information he wanted was by a ruse. He started his inquiries by saying, "We're looking for some information about a couple of our friends who were going fishing with you yesterday," he said.

"We didn't go fishing yesterday," Captain Flont replied quickly.

"Oh, then maybe you were the captain who was over in Smith's woods yesterday," Joe broke in.

Captain Flont's grip tightened on the doorjamb. He scowled, then declared, "I wasn't in any woods. Now get off this boat!"

The Hardy boys held their ground. "How about your man Ragu?" Frank asked. "Was he over there?"

At the mention of his name, Ragu came up behind them. He had picked up a heavy deck mop, and was wielding it as though he might turn it into a formidable weapon. Looking at his captain, the dark-skinned sailor said:

"I was with Captain Flont yesterday. We were on ship's business."

"Now you have your answers," the skipper shouted. "Get off my ship!"

Frank and Joe did not move quickly enough to suit the captain. The captain's shout had aroused the other two crew members who came up from below. They, with the willing help of Ragu, gripped the unwanted callers by the elbows and rushed them off the boat. The boys were thrown forcibly onto the dock.

As the sailors returned to the gangplank, Frank and Joe heard one of them mutter, "It's lucky they didn't show up for the moonlight ride!"

The boys brushed themselves off and walked back to their car. When they were almost home, Joe, still rubbing his bruised hip and black-and-blue arm, said:

"It sure is strange that it takes a captain, a mate, and two crew members to run a fifty-foot fishing cruiser. And what do you think that fellow meant about a moonlight ride?"

"I don't know, but I believe we ought to find out if he meant tonight. There'll be a full moon. Let's take the *Sleuth* out and keep an eye on the *Daisy K*."

At home the boys found a telegram from one of the paper mills. Frank read it and said:

"Joe, did you ever hear of the Mediterranean Steamship Line? The records of this paper company show that the fouled anchor stationery was made for them and is used on all their ships. It was sold through the London office."

Joe said he had never heard of the line, but went to one of his father's bookcases and brought back a paper-covered book containing ships' registries of various countries. He thumbed through it, then halted at one page.

"Here it is," he announced. "Some of their ships ply between New York and the Middle East. Do you want me to check the recent arrivals and departures of any of them?"

"That's a good idea," Frank agreed.

As Joe scanned the shipping news in the *Bayport Times,* he said, "Here's an item on one—the S.S. *Continental.* She arrived in New York early this week. Her normal course would have taken her close to the coast at Bayport. Say, do you think the *Continental* might be the boat that's bringing aliens to the United States?"

"It could be," Frank admitted. "But it might just be a ship on which a member of the gang was traveling."

Determined to track down every possible clue, Frank called the Mediterranean Line's New York office. He explained that the Hardys were detectives, working on a government case, and asked for a list of Indian passengers on recent voyages of their ships to New York. The passenger agent assured him that it would be sent by mail at once, together with any other helpful information the line could give.

"With that co-operation, it sounds as if the company's on the up and up," he remarked to his brother.

Just as the moon was rising that evening, Frank and Joe headed for the *Sleuth,* which was still moored at a neighbor's boathouse. They paused to note the progress of repairs on their own building which had been so badly burned.

"It'll be at least two weeks before we can take the *Sleuth* back," Frank commented.

"Yes, and the firebug who caused the trouble hasn't been apprehended yet," Joe said grimly.

Joe gassed up the *Sleuth* while Frank took the wheel. Soon they were speeding out of Bayport harbor. There were a number of islands near the inlet where they could wait for their quarry. Frank chose one that lay in shadows, cut the motor, and turned off their running lights.

"I feel like one of those falcons 'waiting on' until its prey comes along," Joe remarked with a grin.

In the bright moonlight the boys could see other boats plying up and down the harbor, but all of them were pleasure craft. Finally, however, Frank whispered:

"I think this is it. There's a boat with the *Daisy K*'s lines."

Both boys positively identified Captain Flont's craft as it moved past them. They gave it a reasonable lead, then started after it. The chase continued for about five miles, then the boys noticed the *Daisy K* slowing down. Frank cut the *Sleuth*'s engine.

A few minutes later a large motor dory appeared beyond the fishing boat and pulled alongside. A rope ladder clattered over the rail of Flont's ship and two men scrambled down the rungs into the dory.

As the smaller boat pulled away toward the open sea, the *Daisy K* started up again, turned in a wide arc, and headed back toward Bayport.

"We *must* find out where that dory's going!" Joe said.

The *Sleuth* took up the chase!

CHAPTER XIV

Hunting a Hawk

THE Hardys had been following the mysterious motor dory in their own boat for some time when suddenly the *Sleuth*'s motor began to sputter and the craft lost way.

Joe, seated on the forward deck as lookout, whirled around and asked, "What's the matter?"

"Sounds as if we're out of gas," Frank replied. "Didn't you fill the tank?"

"Of course I did," Joe insisted. "The gauge read full when I stopped pouring."

Frank unscrewed the cap and beamed his flashlight inside. "I have news for you, Joe," he said grimly. "The gauge still reads full, but there isn't a drop of gas in the tank!"

"Well, for Pete's sake!"

The Hardys examined the gauge carefully and discovered that it was jammed.

"This didn't jam by itself," Frank declared. "Someone tampered with it!"

"Think it might have been someone from the *Daisy K?*" Joe asked.

"Could be. But it sure puts a monkey wrench in our plans for tonight."

The motor dory was out of sight by this time. In disgust the boys brought out the emergency fuel can and emptied its contents into the tank. Since there was little hope now of locating the dory, even in the moonlight and with their limited fuel supply, the boys headed for home. While Frank fixed the gauge, they speculated about where the dory had come from. Perhaps from a ship waiting at sea? The boys could see no lights to indicate any vessel, however, and concluded that the dory might be planning to meet a passing ship later.

"I wonder who those two men were who climbed off the *Daisy K,*" Frank said thoughtfully.

Joe shrugged. "I guess our only hope of solving that is to keep the *Daisy K*'s crew under close observation," he commented. "When we get back to town, let's ask one of Dad's operatives to watch them."

"Jeff Kane's in town. He's a good man," Frank suggested.

When the brothers reached Bayport, Frank telephoned the detective. Kane readily agreed to take over the assignment, leaving the boys free to track down their other clues.

Early the next morning, after feeding the falcon.

they took turns phoning the three pet shops which they had not had time to call the day before, plus several in nearby counties. This time they were more successful. Two of the owners supplied them with the names of six carrier-pigeon fanciers. Three of these were in Bayport, while the others were some distance away. With Frank at the wheel of the convertible, the boys started on their quest. The first place was only half a mile from their home. The pigeon keeper, a young man about twenty-five, proved to be a squab breeder who kept a few carrier pigeons as a hobby. He showed them to Frank and Joe.

"I enter these in cross-country races," he said. "It's a swell sport." The pigeon fancier smiled. "My birds have brought me several cups and ribbons," he added, stroking one of the racers fondly.

In reply to a question from Frank, the young man said he had never taken his birds out on the water and released them.

"In fact, I don't know anyone around here who would have reason to," he said, "because the contests are always from inland cities to the coast."

The Hardys thanked him for the information and went on their way. Both of the other local men proved to be above suspicion as well.

The next name on their list was that of a Reed Newton who lived about five miles away. When Frank and Joe reached his home, they found him to be a retired man in late middle age, who had flown pigeons as a hobby for many years. He had a large cote and several breeding cages.

"You raise more pigeons than you train and fly, don't you, Mr. Newton?" Frank asked.

"Oh, yes," the fancier replied. "I sell them." He smiled boyishly. "I may sound a bit vain, but my pigeons are becoming known all over the world."

"Has anyone purchased a large number of birds from you recently?"

Reed Newton wrinkled his brow for some moments, then replied, "Not recently. But about two years ago I had a big order. A young man from India, named Bhagnav, bought a whole flock of pigeons."

"Bhagnav!" Joe exclaimed, but recovered quickly and added, "That's an unusual name."

"Can you describe this man?" Frank asked.

Mr. Newton hesitated, then answered, "Well, as I remember, he was a tall, slender, rather handsome fellow of about twenty-six. One thing I do particularly remember was that he had a scar at the base of his chin. It stood out clearly because it was a slightly lighter shade than the rest of his face."

Frank and Joe could hardly believe their good fortune in picking up this clue. Was the Bhagnav who had purchased the pigeons related to the maharajah's cousin who was now using the name of Delhi?

After the brothers had left Mr. Newton and were on their way to interview the next fancier, they began to speculate about the man named Bhagnav who had bought the pigeons.

"It's possible," said Frank, "that he was an impostor who had planned this smuggling racket as far back as two years ago."

"Right. Figuring that if anyone uncovered the plot, the real Bhagnav would be blamed. We must phone Mr. Delhi about this as soon as we get home."

The drive to the farm of John Fenwick, the last pigeon fancier on the boys' list, took them some time and on the way they stopped at a roadside restaurant to have lunch. During the last part of the journey both boys breathed deeply of the clean country air and enjoyed the verdant rolling landscape. When Joe suddenly spotted a sign reading FENWICK at the foot of a lane, he exclaimed:

"What a weird setup for a pigeon fancier!"

On the lawn inside the cyclone fence that lined the property were several perches. Each of them held a hooded hawk!

"Fenwick must be breeding fighter pigeons!" Frank grinned as he turned the convertible into the driveway.

A pleasant-looking man in his middle thirties strode briskly from the back yard. He was dressed in rough clothing, had on a tight-fitting cap, and held two coils of nylon rope over his arm. At first the Hardys mistook him for a telephone lineman because of the climbing hooks he held in one hand.

"We're looking for John Fenwick," Frank announced.

"I'm your man," he replied, smiling. "What can I do for you?"

"We're interested in your pigeons," Joe said.

Mr. Fenwick laughed and remarked, "You're about two years too late for that. As you can see from the perches on the lawn, I've switched my interest to falconry. It's an exciting sport, particularly if you begin by capturing the young hawks yourself to train."

"We have a peregrine falcon," Joe replied. "That's the reason we came to talk to you. Our falcon brought down a pigeon and we were trying to find the owner so we could settle accounts."

"Fine attitude, son," Mr. Fenwick declared. "Since you're interested in the birds yourself, you might like to come along with me today. I'm going up to Cliff Mountain to get a young hawk from an eyrie—that's a nest—that I've been observing."

Frank and Joe were thrilled at this idea. "If you don't think we'd be in the way, we'd like to!" the older boy said.

"Not at all. In fact, you might be of great service."

Frank suggested that Mr. Fenwick put his gear in their car and let them drive him to Cliff Mountain. He accepted, and as they drove along, he explained that he was particularly interested in duck hawks.

"I spotted one of their nests out on the mountain, and have been watching the tercel and the falcon. The eggs have been hatched now. There were four of them. I will take only one young hawk out of the eyrie and leave the rest to fly away and raise broods of their own. Then, too, the parent birds will return next year to nest again."

When he and the boys arrived at Cliff Mountain, Frank parked the car and Mr. Fenwick led the way up the trail to the precipice that had given the mountain its name. The going was rugged, but the boys' enthusiasm for hawking and adventure spurred them on. When they reached the edge of the shaly cliff, Mr. Fenwick explained how he used his ropes for climbing down the rock face to the eyrie.

He tied a heavy rope around a sturdy oak which seemed to be growing right out of the rocks. The loose end was dropped over the side of the cliff, falling until its entire one hundred and twenty-five feet hung down.

"Usually," Mr. Fenwick explained, "it's a good idea to have a rope that will reach all the way to the bottom of the cliff. Then, if you can't climb back to the top safely, you can at least get to the ground without injury. But this cliff is too high for that. No alternative but to come back up."

The hawk hunter then took a smaller rope and tied a Spanish bowline in it. He stepped into this and tied the loose ends of the rope around his waist to make a sling, which would enable him to rest when he got tired of climbing the heavy vertical rope. It would also protect him from falling if he were hit by a tumbling rock or struck by a hawk.

The Hardys tended the ropes while Mr. Fenwick went over the edge of the cliff. He lowered himself about sixty feet, then called back:

"The mother isn't here, but there are three fledglings. One egg didn't hatch."

The mother hawk was not in sight but Mr. Fenwick called up again, "Keep your eyes open for the mother. She's likely to resist an invasion of her nest. I don't want any trouble, if I can help it. I've been attacked before and it's no fun."

But the falcon did not return and in a few minutes the hawk hunter announced that he had a young bird in his packsack and was coming up. He signaled to be lifted to the rim. As he came over the edge and the rest of the line was pulled up, Mr. Fenwick said:

"Funny, I haven't seen any sign of the tercel, either. Usually he'll do the hunting for food for the young. Then the falcon will take the quarry from him in mid-air, pluck it, and feed the fledglings."

"Do you think someone might have shot the tercel and the falcon is getting the food?" Frank asked.

"That's possible," Mr. Fenwick replied. "And she will have to do all the work herself until the young ones can fly."

Joe, curious to see the nest, asked, "Do you think I could get a look at the hawks in the eyrie?"

"Sure," replied John Fenwick. "You can see them by leaning over the ledge and looking down."

Joe moved along toward a good vantage point,

dropped to his knees, and wriggled to the edge of the cliff.

He was disappointed not to be able to see the young hawks because of a shaly overhang which hid the nest. He inched farther over.

Just then Frank happened to glance up. The mother hawk was banking overhead. The next second she plummeted toward Joe like a rocket!

"Look out! Get back!" Frank screamed.

But there was not time for his brother to pull himself back. The falcon slammed into Joe's head, brushing his face with her talons. As Joe threw up both arms to protect his head, he lost his balance and disappeared over the edge of the cliff!

CHAPTER XV

Chet in Trouble

HORRIFIED at seeing his brother slip off the cliff, Frank ran toward the brink where Joe had been. John Fenwick followed.

But the earth, loosened by Joe's plunge, made the footing unsure and it seemed for a moment as if they too would go over into the chasm. All this time the falcon was circling and screaming overhead.

"Joe!" Frank wailed. "Joe!"

But his brother could not answer. Plunging down the steep face of the cliff, Joe had clutched frantically at roots and vines, only to have them snap off or slip through his fingers.

At last, however, his hands gripped a large tree root. It held, and the muscles in his arms and shoulders jerked painfully as they caught the full force of his descent.

Now, coughing and half blinded from the dust stirred up by his slide, he could only grit his teeth and hang on. Blood from the deep scratches made by the falcon's sharp talons was running down his cheek, and the whole experience had left him weak.

Gradually, however, his strength returned and he looked below. There was a smooth shelf of rock a short distance beneath him and in relief he dropped to it. The overhang of the cliff made it impossible for Frank and Mr. Fenwick to see him without leaning out dangerously over the cliff.

Frantic now, Frank cried, "Joe! Joe!"

"I'm all right!" his brother called back, but a grim smile crossed his face as he watched the mother hawk heading toward her nest and young.

"Where are you?" Frank called down.

"On a ledge below the rim of the cliff."

Moments later Joe saw a lifeline swinging toward him. Because of the cliff's overhang, the rope was a bit beyond his reach, and for a while it looked as though he might still plummet to the depths in trying to reach it. Finally, Joe broke off a length of curling root, and using it for a hook, managed to bring the rope close enough to grasp it.

Quickly he lashed it around his waist and yelled, "Haul away!"

As Frank and Mr. Fenwick pulled hand over hand on the line, Joe braced his legs against the rock wall and literally "walked" up the cliff with their help. When he came up over the edge, Frank gripped the back of Joe's jacket and rolled him to complete safety.

At sight of Joe's blood-covered face, Frank asked in concern, "Are you hurt badly?"

Joe managed a grin. "I guess I look worse than I feel. It's mostly my pride that's hurt. I should have watched for that mother hawk. Thank goodness she finally returned to her nest."

"You learned the hard way," Mr. Fenwick remarked, then pointed out a mountain stream in which Joe could wash the blood from his face. "I feel it was my fault. We're lucky it ended so well."

Joe said, "Forget it. But how about my taking a look at the falcon you brought up? I'd like to see *one* fledgling, anyway!"

The falcon's tail and wing feathers were short because the bird was so young. Small tufts of down clung to them. The young bird's feet were a light greenish gray instead of brilliant orange like the adults'.

Both Frank and Joe noticed how large the feet were. They were already fully grown, even though its feathers were still developing.

The thing that amazed them most was that the young falcon was brownish black instead of blackish blue like their own hawk. Mr. Fenwick explained that the young birds never have the same plumage color and markings as the adults.

"Next spring this bird will begin to molt—that is, drop her old feathers and grow new ones. These will be the adult plumage like your peregrine's."

"Is that true for all hawks?" Joe asked.

"Yes," Mr. Fenwick replied, as he put the young falcon back in the pack to begin the return journey to the Fenwick home.

When they reached there, Mr. Fenwick gave Joe an antiseptic patch to cover the cuts on his face. Then the boys left the falconer, who extended a cordial invitation to return soon.

Back at their own house, they found Sam Radley waiting for them. He was seated in the garden with Mrs. Hardy and Aunt Gertrude. The falcon sat on the perch beside them.

"Good night! What happened to you, Joe?" Radley exclaimed, seeing the boy's swollen cheek with the bandage on it. Mrs. Hardy and Aunt Gertrude expressed horror when told of the accident.

"You might have been killed!" Aunt Gertrude stormed. "There ought to be a law against taking young hawks, then boys like you wouldn't be tempted to do such foolish things!"

Mrs. Hardy examined the wounds but felt that no further treatment was necessary. "Nature will take care of it now," she said.

As Radley began his report, the two women arose and went into the house.

"No one returned to the hunting lodge and I doubt that anyone will, since they'll figure it's being watched. I did learn something of importance, though. As I was leaving Smith's woods, I met Mr. Morton. He asked me to give you this message. Mr. Smith's lawyer told him that the woods were leased for the summer to a dark-skinned man by the name of Sutter. I have a feeling the name is a phony and that we'll find he's one of our Indian boys."

Frank and Joe whistled. This was indeed important information!

At that moment a special-delivery letter arrived for the boys from the Mediterranean Line. It stated that no Indians had arrived on any of their vessels' recent trips to New York.

"This information may interest you, however," the letter went on. "A couple of years ago there was an Indian member of the *Continental*'s crew named Bangalore. He jumped ship. This company is particularly disturbed, because the Immigration authorities hold us responsible for such things."

As he folded the letter, Frank said, "I wonder if we could get a photograph of this Bangalore. Maybe we could dig one up through the steamship company."

"I'll try to locate one," Radley offered.

Frank then told Radley of the clue picked up from Mr. Newton about the pigeon fancier using the name Bhagnav, and the boys' decision to phone Mr. Delhi about it. Joe put in a long-distance call, but there was no answer at Mr. Ghapur's home, where the emissary was staying.

"Well, anything more I can do for you boys?" Radley asked. "Of course I'll continue to keep an eye on the lodge."

Frank and Joe could think of nothing else. They

mentioned Kane's shadowing the *Daisy K*'s crew and that they expected a report from him soon.

"And I think we should talk to the Coast Guard," Frank remarked.

"I did that while I was waiting for you," Radley said. "The local men have found nothing suspicious on boats or ships in the area they cover. Of course they don't go out too far beyond the twelve-mile limit. Does that suggest anything to you?"

"You bet it does!" Joe spoke up. "For one thing, it seems to back up our idea that a large steamer anchors offshore, receives some sort of signal—or maybe sends its own message by carrier pigeon. Then the smuggled Indians are taken off in boats like the motor dory we trailed last night."

"But why couldn't the Coast Guard fly out there and spot such a transfer?" Frank pointed out. "Then, when the dory reaches our waters, it could be nabbed."

"I suppose they might," Radley agreed. "But if the smuggled Indians swam a distance from a large ship to the smaller boat at night, the Coast Guard sure would have trouble spotting them."

"And it's impossible for them to cover every bit of shore line along Bayport at once," Frank added with a grin, "especially at night when a dory could slip in. It might even be that the aliens swim in the last half mile."

After Radley left, Frank and Joe talked over their

next move. "I suggest that we use Miss Peregrine for a little sleuthing," Frank said.

"How?"

"Let's take the falcon out to Chet's farm and have George Simons meet us there with his copter. It's a shorter drive for us there than to the airport and maybe Chet would like to go along. We'll go up in the egg beater and keep watch for a pigeon coming from the ocean and heading southwest. If we spot one, we'll follow it until the bird starts down to its cote. Then we'll turn the falcon loose and let her trail the pigeon right to its cote. That way we ought to be able to locate the hide-out, and also intercept any message it may be carrying."

"You mean we'll kill two clues with one bird?" Joe grinned, then added, "What say we try it right now?"

"You feel okay?"

"Sure."

Frank first phoned Chet, who said, "Count me in. I sure would like to go along."

Then Frank called George Simons, who agreed to meet them at the Morton farm in half an hour. Joe got the hawk's equipment, hooded and wristed her, and the boys drove off. When they reached the farm, the helicopter was already settling in an open area behind the barn. The boys headed for it at once to tell Simons their plan.

Chet, seeing them from the kitchen window, came

outside and followed them. As he ambled past a corner of the barn, a masked figure moved up behind him. Before Chet could whirl around, his arms were pinned behind his back and a hand was clamped over his mouth!

In a low, fierce whisper, the masked man ordered, "Bring that falcon to your barn and leave it there. If you don't, you and the Hardys will be in serious trouble! And don't tell anyone why you're doing it!"

Violently Chet squirmed and twisted in the grasp of his assailant but could not free himself.

"Agree!" the man hissed. "Agree quickly, or it will go hard with you—and even harder with the Hardys!"

CHAPTER XVI

A Ruse

THE masked man tightened his grip and repeated the threat.

"Listen, fat boy! Get that hawk if you value your life and the Hardys'!"

Chet wanted to tackle the man but figured that there might be a second man in hiding. He told himself that after all the falcon was not so important as his friends' safety! Certainly the helicopter could go anywhere the falcon could.

"All right," he finally agreed. "I'll do it."

The masked man pushed Chet along until they were close to a small door in the barn. Then he turned him loose and darted into the darkness of the barn, closing the door behind him.

For a moment Chet was tempted not to heed the order, but for his friends' sakes he decided to carry through. He headed toward the Hardys with trembling legs. As Frank and Joe explained their plans to Simons, Chet interrupted to say:

"Sounds swell. M-mind if I hold the f-falcon on the trip?"

"But the bird isn't accustomed to you," Frank said. "She wouldn't respond to your commands."

"Well, can't I at least h-hold her until you s-spot the pigeon?" Chet pleaded.

Frank and Joe exchanged puzzled glances. They both sensed something was wrong with Chet, for he was not usually so nervous.

"That wouldn't work too well, either," Frank told him.

Chet cast an anxious glance over his shoulder in the direction of the barn, then stared at the hooded falcon. She was standing quietly on Joe's gauntlet. He was checking the jesses to make certain that they were firmly fastened to the bird's legs. Then he un-snapped the swivel hook, so that he could release the falcon quickly.

Suddenly Chet dived at Joe and grabbed for the bird! With a startled cry, Joe stepped back and the falcon flapped her wings to hold her balance.

Frank clutched the stout boy's arm. "What's wrong with you, Chet? You act as though you're crazy! This bird can be ruined if she's disturbed. You mustn't make a pass at her like that! Move gently and slowly or she will bate off the hand."

Finally Chet decided that the Hardy boys would have to know of the threat. He glanced again at the barn, then said in a hoarse whisper:

"L-listen, fellows. A masked man stopped me at the barn a couple of minutes ago and ordered me to get the falcon from you. He told me to leave it inside the barn. If I don't, your lives and mine won't be worth a plugged nickel!"

Simons, who had heard Chet's explanation, leaned out of the cockpit in amazement and said:

"Whew! Trouble! Can I help?"

Frank and Joe were grim, realizing that the only way out was by a ruse.

"You sure can help," Frank told the pilot. "We'll give the hawk to Chet. He can take his time about getting it to the barn. In the meantime, Joe and I will pretend we've gone off with you in the copter, but we'll sneak out the other side, double back, and try to nab this guy and anybody who might be with him."

Joe took the gauntlet from his wrist, handed it to Chet, and helped him put it on. Then he switched the falcon to the youth's wrist and handed him the end of the leash. In a loud voice he called "Good luck!" as though Chet had asked to borrow the hawk for an afternoon's hunting.

Simons jumped to the ground and the Hardys entered the passenger compartment. Then, while Chet and the pilot stood close together beside the helicopter to cut off any view from underneath the craft, Frank and Joe quickly slipped out the window on the far side and took cover in back of some raspberry bushes. From there they made their way toward the barnyard fence as the helicopter rose and headed toward the woods.

Chet, who had started for the barn, was having trouble with the falcon. She bobbed up and down on his wrist, turned toward the throbbing sound of the rotors on the helicopter, and flew out to the end of the leash several times.

Chet, however, managed to get her to the barn, roll open the big door, and place the bird inside.

"Pretty rough on the hawk," Frank whispered to Joe. "But I guess Chet is scared plenty."

The frightened boy turned and hurried to the house. After he had climbed the rear steps and slammed the screen door to the kitchen behind him, the masked man slipped furtively out of the barn with the hawk under one arm.

Instantly the Hardys were upon him, and at a shrill whistle from Joe, Chet dashed back on the double. As Joe took the hawk, Frank pinned the prisoner to the ground and ripped off his mask.

Ragu! For a few seconds the first mate from the *Daisy K* stared insolently at the boys, then lowered his eyes.

"Well," said Frank grimly, as he let the sailor up but kept hold of him, "suppose you talk."

"What do you want me to say? I got your bird, but you caught me. I'll go quiet!"

"Oh, no, you won't," Chet growled. "You threatened me and the Hardys."

"That was just to make you get the hawk," Ragu answered, watching Joe sullenly as he took the gauntlet from Chet and wristed the falcon.

"I know someone who will pay me well for a trained bird. I'm in debt. I need the money," Ragu went on.

"You'll have to give a better reason than that," Frank told him. "How did you know we would have the falcon out here?"

"I—I was near your back yard this afternoon and overheard you make plans to bring the hawk here."

"Keep talking," Joe said grimly.

"I've told you all I know," the sailor insisted.

"It will go easier with you if you tell the truth," Frank said. "What do you know about the smuggling and kidnaping rackets that are going on around here?"

Ragu winced but remained silent. Joe burst out, "I'm sure you can tell plenty about Captain Flont and the *Daisy K.*"

The sailor gave a nervous twitch. "Let me go!" he shouted. "I don't know anything."

The boys marched their prisoner to the kitchen porch. Frank and Joe kept a close watch on him while Chet went to phone Chief Collig.

"Tell him," Frank said, "that we have a prisoner for him. He can book Ragu for assault on you today and Joe a week ago, and attempted robberies of the falcon. If Collig can't get a confession out of him, we'll call in the FBI."

At the mention of Federal authorities, Ragu visibly slumped. But it was obvious that his lips had been sealed, probably by fear.

The group waited until they saw the Bayport patrol car turning into the Morton driveway. Then, with Frank and Chet holding their prisoner firmly by the arms, they started toward the police car.

Chief Collig and Patrolman Smuff climbed out of the car. As they eyed the hawk, Frank explained the circumstances of the arrest, and told Smuff that Ragu was the "deeply tanned" thief they had been looking for.

Before Smuff or the chief had a chance to reply, Frank suddenly cried out:

"Joe, there's a pigeon! It's winging from the same direction as the other pigeons we've spotted. Let the hawk loose!"

Hearing this, Ragu tore himself free from the grip of Patrolman Smuff and dashed toward Joe and the hunting hawk. He snatched at the leash but was quickly subdued. When he began to rave and rant like a wild man, the Hardys were sure Ragu must know that the pigeon was carrying a message or more rubies!

Joe unhooded the falcon, which spotted the pigeon, took off into the air, and climbed toward it.

Meanwhile, Ragu continued to cry out oaths in both English and a foreign tongue. Frank commented on his actions to the police and added:

"Chief, I'm sure Ragu is guilty of a lot more than he's admitting."

"I'll keep him in jail until he talks," the officer said.

"We'll be in to prefer charges against him sometime tonight," Frank said.

"Good enough," Chief Collig agreed.

Smuff hustled Ragu into the patrol car and the three rode away. Frank and Chet whirled around then and tried to spot the falcon.

Joe, hands shading his eyes, was following the flight of the bird. The peregrine and its prey had moved off over the wooded area and a moment later the pigeon was lost to view.

The Hardys' hearts sank. Had the pigeon escaped?

CHAPTER XVII

Intercepted Ransom

"THE hawk mustn't lose that pigeon!" Joe cried.

As the boys stared hopefully, the peregrine poised for a second, then dived like a miniature rocket. At once Frank, Joe, and Chet ran across the fields, their eyes still following the hawk.

Suddenly, through a rift in the trees, they could see both birds.

"The hawk's got her!" Frank cried a moment later, as both birds dropped into the woods.

"Come on!" Joe shouted gleefully, starting to run.

All three boys fully expected to locate at once the spot where the pigeon and hawk had fallen. When they did not immediately find them, Chet and the Hardys spread out and searched the bushes for some time, but without success.

"Do you think the hawk carried the pigeon off?" Chet asked.

"I doubt it," Frank replied. "That's not usually what a hawk does."

"Then your falcon's got to be here some place," Chet said.

The next moment they heard the whirring of the helicopter and hurried to a clearing, where they could spot the aircraft. They saw Simons, his helicopter window slid back, beckoning for them to follow him.

The boys nodded and moved along the edge of the woods, guided by their friend in the sky. Presently he turned the craft and flew directly over the trees. Now Simons whirled up, then lowered quickly.

Frank interpreted the maneuver. "Simons is trying to tell us the birds are right around here."

Joe held out his gloved hand and whistled sharply. There was a movement in the brush a few yards ahead of the boys. Then they spotted the peregrine falcon and her quarry.

The younger Hardy moved in slowly and picked up the falcon and the mangled pigeon. The boys were sobered by the sight, but in a moment shook off the mood and Chet asked:

"Why don't you fellows feed your bird at home?"

"This time she earned a meal," Joe said, spotting a telltale red container fastened to one of the pigeon's legs.

Frank removed the capsule and opened it. As he shook it gently, two rubies fell out into his hand.

"More ransom payments!" he declared.

"Looks as though you're right," Chet said in awe.

Excitedly the three boys headed back toward the Morton farm. The helicopter was still hovering overhead when they came out into the clearing. As Simons brought it down low, Joe held up the hawk and waved their thanks. Then the pilot headed for the airport to keep another appointment.

When Frank and Joe reached their car they said good-by to Chet and drove home. After putting the falcon in the garage and setting the alarm, the boys went indoors. A message was waiting for them from Jeff Kane, their father's operative. He had shadowed the captain and crew members of the *Daisy K*, and had investigated their reputations, but could find nothing suspicious in their activities. He learned that Captain Flont ruled them with an iron hand and they seemed to fear him.

"If anything crooked is going on," Frank said to Joe, "it's well concealed, that's sure."

Joe put through another call to the home of Rahmud Ghapur, who answered at once. When the Hardys informed him that they had made two important discoveries for Mr. Delhi, the importer asked that the boys not reveal them on the phone.

"I'll pass along your message to Mr. Delhi," Ghapur promised. "He'll probably want to fly up to Bayport sometime tonight."

"We'll be waiting for him."

The Indian arrived about eight o'clock, and as before, he and the boys went up to Mr. Hardy's study. As the maharajah's cousin settled himself in a chair, Frank unwrapped the two rubies and explained how the Hardys had gotten them. Mr. Delhi examined them, then finally said:

"These are very valuable gems and cut exactly like some of the ransom rubies. I could almost swear that they are part of those payments. This poses a serious problem."

He looked from one boy to the other and they felt that something had displeased him. "I do not want to seem ungrateful," Delhi said, "but if these are part of the ransom, and are not received by the fiends who are holding Prince Tava, he may come to harm. You did not realize this phase of the matter, I am sure."

Frank and Joe were thunderstruck. They had not thought of this angle!

"I'm afraid we didn't," Frank replied. "But we may be close enough to these kidnapers to catch them before they attempt anything drastic."

The Hardys told Delhi of the lodge in the woods and the possible flight of the prince with his captors.

Then Frank showed him the sandalwood scent box which Ahmed had found at the lodge. Tenderly, Delhi cupped the box in his hands.

"My new friends," he said with emotion, "you have made a wonderful discovery. This box was given Prince Tava by the maharajah at a ceremony I witnessed myself several years ago. May I keep it now?"

"Of course," Frank replied.

"It—it brings back such happy memories. And Prince Tava will be so delighted when I return it to him."

Delhi stopped and his expression changed abruptly. "This hunting lodge," he said, "you have someone watching it at all times?"

The Hardys reassured him on this point. Then they concluded with the story of the man who had purchased carrier pigeons from Mr. Newton under the name Bhagnav.

"My name!" Delhi exclaimed in amazement. "But not one of my relatives has ever been in this country."

"We thought he was an impostor," Frank said.

"What did this man look like?" Delhi asked.

"We were told he was tall, slender, handsome— about twenty-six years of age. He had a scar under his chin which stood out because it was lighter than the skin on the rest of his face."

The Indian nobleman weighed this information, his brow furrowed. Then he pursed his lips and said, "The description sounds vaguely familiar. But it is not someone with whom I have been in regular contact. I shall speak to my friend Ghapur about this. Perhaps he will recognize the man. In any case, I'm sure the impostor is an enemy, trying to discredit my family's name."

Joe changed the subject. "Does the name Ragu mean anything to you?" he asked.

Mr. Delhi thought this over, then said no. "Can you describe him?" he asked.

But the description of a swarthy, short, heavy-set man did not help.

Frank said, "Ragu works here on a fishing boat called the *Daisy K.* Right now, though, he is in our local jail. We promised to go there tonight and prefer charges. Will you come with us and see if you know Ragu?"

"I shall be glad to go," he said. "But I suggest, in case we should be followed, that we try to throw off any pursuers."

Driving to police headquarters that night, Frank took every precaution to be sure that no one trailed them.

They learned, when they arrived, that Chief Collig was at home for a late dinner, but would return in a few minutes. The sergeant on duty assisted them in filing charges against Ragu. When the boys explained the reason for Mr. Delhi's presence, he took the callers down to the cell where Ragu was being held. On the way he said that the prisoner had refused to admit anything.

When Ragu saw the Hardys, his face twisted into a snarl. He was about to say something, but suddenly his glance rested upon Mr. Delhi. A look of awe and fright spread over his face and he staggered backward.

"It's Prince Bhagnav of Hatavab!" he almost screamed.

Mr. Delhi gazed at the prisoner, who seemed hypnotized that a nobleman of his country had come to see him.

The prince said to the boys, "I do not know this fellow, but evidently he recognizes me from newspaper photographs or public functions."

Following up the advantage of the prisoner's discomfiture, Frank asked him whether he was ready to talk. Ragu acted as if he had not heard the boy. Glassy-eyed, he dropped to his knees and touched his forehead to the floor before the nobleman's feet.

Mr. Delhi spoke to the sailor in his native tongue and Ragu climbed to his feet. As he seated himself on a corner of his bunk, Chief Collig arrived. After the police chief was introduced to Prince Bhagnav, the boys turned the ransom rubies over to the officer for safekeeping.

When Ragu saw the gems he gasped but made no comment.

The police chief then ordered the jailer to unlock the cell door. They all went inside. Forming an arc about the prisoner, they began to question him.

Ragu remained defiant and unco-operative, but the Hardys felt he was almost frightened enough to make a full confession.

Chief Collig asked him to give the reason for his attempted thefts of the falcon and the threats to Chet and the Hardys, then added, "And tell us all you know about the operations of the *Daisy K.*"

Again the mention of Flont's ship had a visible

effect on the first mate. Eyes wide, he stared at Chief Collig for a long moment. Then, abruptly, his shoulders sagged and he looked at the floor.

All further questions about Captain Flont or the *Daisy K* aroused no response.

Finally, Mr. Delhi went directly to the crux of the matter and asked Ragu probing questions about the smuggling of aliens from India into the United States, and more particularly about the kidnaping of Prince Tava.

Ragu looked up, eyes flashing, and uttered one brief phrase. Mr. Delhi nodded, then turned to the others.

"Ragu wishes to talk to me alone," he said.

The boys and the police chief left the cell and waited at the end of the corridor.

Ten minutes later Mr. Delhi called, "It is settled."

When the others returned to the cell, Mr. Delhi said, "Ragu has convinced me that he knows only a little about what is going on. But he is willing to tell us that much."

The Hardys listened in eager anticipation. A break in the case at last!

CHAPTER XVIII

Attack in the Night

CHIEF COLLIG called in a police stenographer to take down Ragu's statement. As Mr. Delhi nodded to Ragu, the *Daisy K*'s first mate began his story.

"First, I know nothing about any smuggling of my countrymen into the United States. I—I did join the group that was planning a kidnaping. But you must believe me—I did not know until too late that Prince Tava was to be the victim. I thought it was a rich Indian businessman, who would never miss the money."

"Prince or businessman, it was a criminal act," the police chief said severely. "Just what was your part in it?"

"A very small one," Ragu insisted. "I ran errands. Once I took a letter from a man that came to our ship. He told me to deliver it to the Bayport Hotel."

"What was the name of the man who came to the *Daisy K?*" Chief Collig broke in.

"I do not know his name," Ragu said emphatically. "The man at the hotel was called Mr. Louis."

Delhi and the police chief glanced at the Hardys for some sign as to whether this name was familiar to them. Frank nodded, remembering the mysterious "L" mentioned in the note one of the pigeons carried.

"How did you expect to get paid for the job, if you didn't know the name of the man who hired you?" Frank asked Ragu.

"He promised to pay me with a ruby ring. It was left in a secret place," Ragu replied. "The only time I wore it was when I came to your house to take the falcon. After that, I was afraid and sold the ring. You know about that."

Frank confirmed this, then Joe asked, "Who hired you to steal our falcon?"

"I don't know that, either," Ragu persisted. "I got a phone call at my rooming house. An unfamiliar voice said if I could steal the falcon, I would receive another ruby in payment. I tried twice but failed."

"What part do the pigeons play in this racket?" Frank asked Ragu.

"They carry messages, but I don't know where they go. And I don't know what the notes say."

Chief Collig turned to Mr. Delhi and asked him if he had any further questions. The maharajah's cousin said he had none.

Frank spoke up. "Ragu, tell us about Captain

Flont and his activities. He's more than a fishing boat captain, isn't he?"

Ragu bit his lip. He looked at Mr. Delhi, then settled back on his cot.

"I don't know much about Captain Flont," he said. "I've only worked for him a short time."

All further questioning Ragu answered with a shrug. No amount of persuasion would unlock the first mate's lips. It was evident, as Kane had learned, that the crew of the *Daisy K* was afraid of their captain.

"I guess we've found out all we can tonight," said Chief Collig as the visitors left the cell. "After the stenographer types up that statement and Ragu signs it, there'll be plenty of evidence to present to the grand jury."

"I suggest," said Mr. Delhi, "that since Ragu recognized me, he have no visitors."

"Don't worry about that, sir," Collig said. "There are certain procedures that will have to be taken care of and that will require at least forty-eight hours."

On the way back to the Hardy home Mr. Delhi was silent, but just before they turned into the Hardy driveway, he asked, "How will you boys proceed now? When Captain Flont hears of Ragu's arrest he may make trouble."

"We'll have to take that chance," Joe replied. Then he snapped his fingers. "Frank, what say you and I disguise ourselves as elderly sportsmen and join a fishing party on the *Daisy K* for a day?"

"You mean to do some detecting?"

"Right."

Joe decided to take the falcon indoors for the night. Ragu's arrest might mean trouble, as Mr. Delhi had suggested. At any rate, the smugglers would be doubly determined to get the falcon. Frank agreed that the hawk should be given extra protection.

Mr. Delhi followed the boys through the kitchen door and into the living room where Mrs. Hardy and Aunt Gertrude were reading.

While Joe took the hawk to his room, Frank presented their visitor to the women. The boys' mother smilingly said, "Mr. Delhi, it's much too late for you to start back for Washington. We should like to have you spend the night with us."

"I'm grateful for your thoughtfulness," the Indian nobleman declared. "Thank you. I will accept."

Aunt Gertrude left the room but returned in a few minutes with a tray containing cookies, coffee, and milk. Mr. Delhi smiled and said:

"This is what you Americans call a midnight snack, is it not?"

"Even when it's served at ten o'clock," Mrs. Hardy said, her eyes twinkling.

By eleven o'clock the boys and their visitor found it impossible to keep from yawning, despite the interesting conversation on the differences in customs between India and the United States. Mrs. Hardy suggested that they retire if they wished.

"I shall wait for my husband," she said. "He'll reach here about midnight."

The boys were pleased to hear that their father was coming and would have liked to talk to him as soon as he arrived. But they were very sleepy, and also they had to rise early for the fishing trip.

Kissing their mother and Aunt Gertrude good night, they laughingly reminded Mrs. Hardy to set the burglar alarm, then escorted their visitor to the guest room. The brothers provided him with pajamas, robe, and slippers.

The robe and pajamas looked as if they would be about the right size. But Frank and Joe could not help laughing at the expression of consternation on the Indian's face when he tried on the slippers.

Mr. Delhi chuckled. "I am afraid I shall—how do you say it?—*swim* in these!"

This remark brought fresh gales of laughter from the boys, and Frank said, grinning, "Joe, I never knew you had such big feet!"

"What do you mean?" Joe replied with mock indignation. "Those are an extra pair I got from your closet!"

Still laughing, the three said good night and within half an hour Frank and Joe were sound asleep. But some time later, Frank awoke with a

The hooded figure froze, blinded by the glare.

start. He glanced at the luminous dial of their alarm clock. It was almost two o'clock.

Joe awoke a moment later and called from his bed, "What's the matter? Is it time to get ready for the fishing trip already?"

"No, it's only two o'clock. But do you hear someone moving around downstairs?" Frank asked.

"No."

"An intruder couldn't be in the house," Frank mused. "Mother and Dad would have set the burglar alarm before going to bed."

Joe left his bed and tiptoed across to the door. He opened it and listened for several seconds.

"Not a sound," he reported.

"That's good," Frank replied, stretching and relaxing again. "Now let's go back to sleep."

Joe closed the bedroom door, then walked over to the side window and opened it wider. As he did, he saw something move on the lawn.

"Psst—Frank! Come here quick!"

His brother was at his side in a second.

"What's up?" Frank asked.

"Someone's down at the edge of the lawn," Joe said. "Over by the hedge."

"Let's throw the spotlights on him," the older boy suggested.

The Hardy home had a bright spotlight under the eaves on each side of the house—a precaution occasioned by too many prowlers interested in the detectives' work. The lights were controlled from switches in the upper and lower halls.

"Okay," Joe agreed.

Frank dashed from the room to snap on the switch. Instantly the front lawn was flooded with light. Outlined against the hedge was a hooded figure with one arm raised above its head. In that position, it froze for a moment, evidently blinded by the glare.

"Looks as if he was going to throw something!" Frank whispered, rejoining his brother at the window.

Before Joe could make a reply, the strange figure hurled a large, round object straight toward the boys.

Involuntarily they stepped back, but the man missed his mark and the object crashed into a side window of the living room directly below them.

Instantly the burglar alarm clanged, then was drowned out in a deafening roar! The spotlights went out and the Hardy home shuddered on its foundation!

Frank and Joe were flung violently to the floor!

CHAPTER XIX

Doubting a Friend

DAZED and puzzled by the explosion in their home, Joe Hardy picked himself up in the pitch-dark bedroom and groped about.

"Frank, you okay?" he asked.

There was no reply. Fearful, Joe felt around the floor for his brother but could not locate him. Bumping into the bureau which had been shifted out of place by the impact, Joe opened the top drawer and found a flashlight.

Its beam revealed Frank's unconscious form between the beds.

"His head must have hit the bedpost," Joe decided as he knelt beside his brother.

Suddenly Frank stirred, opened his eyes, and tried to get to his feet.

"What? Where—?" he asked, falling back still dazed.

"Our house was bombed," Joe told him. "Are you all right now?"

"Y-yes," Frank replied weakly, his right hand going to the back of his head. With Joe's assistance he got up. "How are the folks and Mr. Delhi?" he asked.

"I don't know. We'd better find out pronto."

As he opened the door to the hall, a wave of acrid smoke rolled toward the boys. Through it, Joe could see his father with a flashlight coming toward them.

"Is everybody all right?" Joe called.

"Your mother is. I don't know about the others. We'd better check."

Behind him, they could now see Mrs. Hardy and a moment later Aunt Gertrude's door flew open. Relieved that her family was safe, she pointed toward the guest-room door.

"There's your trouble!" she cried out. "If we weren't entertaining all kinds of strange visitors, things like this wouldn't happen. Respectable people have *no* business getting mixed up with such folks!" She began to sneeze and cough.

"You are right, Miss Hardy," said a voice through the smoke, which had begun to clear. Mr. Delhi walked out of his room and came toward the group. "I am without doubt responsible for what has happened. Apparently my identity is known to my enemies, regardless of our precautions last evening. From now on, I shall come out into the open and strike back at them myself. I cannot subject good people like yourselves to further danger. I am relieving you from the case at once. You have already suffered a great deal in trying to help me and my country."

"Oh!" cried Aunt Gertrude. "Forgive me, sir. I didn't mean—"

Mr. Hardy looked first at his sister, then at their guest. "Mr. Delhi," he said, "we will see this thing through with you. We cannot bow out of a case—especially one that is so near a solution."

"And I don't believe," Joe spoke up, "that the bomb was thrown into our house because of you, Mr. Delhi. I saw the fellow aim it directly at Frank and me as we stood in our bedroom window."

Just then a voice at the foot of the stairs called, "Anyone up there hurt?"

They looked over the stair railing and in the beams from Mr. Hardy's flashlight saw the anxious face of the night patrolman on the Elm Street beat.

"Everyone's all right," the detective assured him. "We'll be right down."

He and the boys hurriedly put on robes and ran downstairs to investigate the damage to their house and to make sure a fire had not started. There was no sign of a blaze, but they were horrified at what they saw! Part of one wall in the living room gaped open and the room was a shambles.

By this time a crowd of neighbors had gathered. All of them offered their sympathy and the accommodations of their homes for as long as the Hardys wished to stay.

"Thank you," Mr. Hardy said to each one, "but since the damage is so extensive, I believe we'd better move to the Bayport Hotel. It looks as though it will be several weeks before our home will be habitable again."

Joe proposed to his father that he and Frank stay at the house to guard it from pilferers.

Mr. Hardy smiled. "You boys will be needed for sleuthing elsewhere," he told his sons. "I'll put Jeff Kane here, together with a few regulars the police will assign. Joe, go tell the others the plan. And insist that Mr. Delhi go with us to the hotel."

Joe relayed the message and Mr. Delhi said he would accompany them and stay at least for the remainder of the night.

After everyone had dressed, and the Hardys had packed a few clothes, they gathered outdoors.

Chief Collig was on hand now, having been summoned from his home. He had ordered searchlights set up and had stationed men on every side of the Hardy house.

The chief reported that the hard ground had yielded no footprints and that his men had found not a single clue to the person who had thrown the bomb. However, in the living room they had found parts of the bomb scattered about. The remnants had been gathered up for the police laboratory to examine.

Satisfied that the situation was under control, Mr.

Hardy and the others went to the Bayport Hotel. Dawn was breaking when they were finally settled in their suite.

By that time all desire for sleep had vanished for everyone except Mr. Hardy. The detective said he had worked late the previous two nights and needed a few hours' rest before tackling several important problems. Not the least of these was the attempt on the lives of himself, his family, and their visitor.

After he had gone to bed, his sons talked with Mr. Delhi for some time about the mystery. But they could not figure out any lead to the identity of the hooded figure who had thrown the bomb. It was certainly not Ragu, since he was safely behind bars in the Bayport jail.

When the hotel coffee shop opened at six o'clock, the three went in to have breakfast. Halfway through the meal, Mr. Delhi excused himself to make a phone call. After several minutes, he returned, much disturbed.

"Forgive me," he began nervously. "I have just learned that I must fly to New York at once. Should you want to reach me, call Mr. Ghapur. He will know of my whereabouts. And please make my apologies to your family."

"Let us drive you to the airport," Frank offered.

The Indian, who seemed extremely upset, said quickly, "Thank you, no. You have been most kind to me. I shall take a cab. Good-by."

With that, he strode out the door of the coffee

shop, the boys following him to the hotel entrance. As he climbed into a brown-and-white cab, they waved farewell to the royal gentleman who had suddenly begun to act so mysteriously.

"What do you suppose upset him so?" Joe said quizzically as they returned to the coffee shop.

"He sure acted strange," Frank agreed, but could not guess the reason.

When the boys finished eating, Frank suggested that they go back to their house to make a search for a clue to the person who had thrown the bomb, in the hope that the police might have overlooked it.

It was shortly after seven when they turned into Elm Street. The story of the explosion had spread all over Bayport, and scores of people had gathered outside the police lines. One of the officers approached the Hardys and said:

"There's a young fellow over there by the barrier who says you boys would want to see him."

Frank, turning, saw Chet waving at them excitedly and asked the officer to let him through. Chet hurried to the boys, his eyes popping as he studied the damage to their home.

"Gee, fellows, I'm sorry this happened," he said. "Is everybody all right?" At a nod from Joe, he went on, "How'd Miss Peregrine take it?"

Frank's and Joe's mouths dropped open. In the excitement they had completely forgotten the prize bird!

They dashed up the porch steps two at a time and

ran pell-mell up the stairway. There was only a slim chance that the falcon would still be alive. The door to their room stood ajar and one glance inside revealed the bird's perch lying in a corner.

But the falcon was gone!

After the first shock was over, Joe said:

"She couldn't have flown away, Frank. Her leash was fastened to the ring at the base of the perch stand. It would have to be twisted or broken to free her. Someone took her!"

Frank nodded. "With all the police and bystanders around here, someone must have seen who it was. Let's go and ask them."

By this time Chet had caught up to the boys and was saying, "What ails you guys? I ask you a simple question and you act as if you'd been shot." When the boys explained, the stout boy said thoughtfully, "Maybe the house was bombed so those smugglers could get your bird."

"That might have been part of the plan," Frank conceded, but he felt sure that there was much more behind it than that.

The three boys headed back downstairs. They checked with Jeff Kane and the policemen guarding the house, but none of them had seen the bird, nor had any one of them entered the house since the second shift of men had come on duty at seven o'clock.

"Let's ask some of the people in the crowd if they saw anyone carry off the bird," Joe suggested.

The boys separated and began quizzing the by-standers. Finally a neighbor woman approached Frank and said:

"I saw your falcon. About six forty-five this morning a man in a taxi came up and spoke to the policeman on duty at the front door. He went upstairs with him and they came down a few minutes later with the falcon. The man drove off in the taxi-cab with it."

"Which policeman was it?" Frank asked.

"I don't see him around just now, so I guess he's gone off duty. But I remember his badge number. It was eighty-two."

"Did you notice what kind of taxicab the man who took the bird came in?" the boy asked.

"It was a brown-and-white cab of the Bayport Taxi Company, I think."

Frank thanked the woman for her information and relayed it to Joe and Chet. Then they climbed into Chet's jalopy and drove to police headquarters.

They traced the officer through the badge number and learned that he was at his home. Frank reached him by phone. The man said that the stranger had told him the Hardys wanted him to get the falcon, and he knew just which room the bird was in.

"No, he didn't give his name," the policeman said. "He was dark-skinned and seemed to be in an awful hurry."

The Hardys were astonished. Dark-skinned man. Brown-and-white cab. Taking the falcon during the time they were finishing breakfast. It all seemed to piece together—unfortunately. Could Mr. Delhi have taken the falcon? Had his phone call to New York prompted this? He certainly had started to act strangely all of a sudden.

As Frank started to ask the policeman for a fuller description of the thief, the connection was broken. He was about to call the officer again when Joe suggested that they get it from the taxi driver, as well as information on his passenger's destination.

The boys headed for the office of the Bayport Taxi Company, a modern outfit with a fleet of radio-equipped taxis. Convinced of the importance of the Hardys' request, the dispatcher willingly contacted his various drivers.

The one they sought appeared at the office about ten minutes later. Frank explained about the missing falcon and their desire to apprehend the thief. The taxi driver's eyebrows went up.

"I remember the guy all right," he said. "I picked him up in front of the Bayport Hotel between six thirty and seven this morning.

"After the man collected the falcon from a house on Elm Street," the driver went on, "he ordered me to drive him down to a deserted wharf on the waterfront. I was curious about why he wanted to go there at that hour of the morning. But this guy claimed that someone was going to pick him up in a boat."

"Could you give us a description of this man?" Frank asked excitedly.

The taxi driver furrowed his brow for a moment, then replied, "Well, he was young and good-looking and dark-skinned, like one of them Indian rug makers down at Ahmed's place. And he had a light scar on his chin. I mean a scar that really stood out—looked lighter than the rest of his skin."

Frank exchanged glances with Joe. They both heaved a sigh of relief. The falcon thief was not Mr. Delhi after all! It must have been the Indian who had bought pigeons from Mr. Newton two years before—the imposter who had used Mr. Delhi's real name of Bhagnav!

The driver noticed the boys' amazed expressions and asked, "Does that description help you?"

"It sure does," Frank said. "Thanks a lot. Now will you drive us to the wharf where you left this man? He may still be there."

The three boys climbed into the cab. Moments later the driver let them out on one of the wharves, promising to wait. They hurried down the length of the dock, but the dark-skinned man was not in sight, and no one they questioned on the small boats tied up at the dock had seen anyone carrying a hooded hawk.

"Looks like a dead end," Joe declared, disappointment in his voice.

Frank agreed, but Chet tried to cheer them up, saying:

"Listen, fellows, you're due for a real break. Wait and see!"

The boys smiled at Chet's loyalty and Frank said, "Let's head back to the hotel and brief Dad on this latest development. He ought to be awake by now."

The taxi driver took them back to Chet's jalopy and Chet in turn drove the Hardys to pick up their car at their home. Then Joe and Frank headed for the hotel.

The three adults listened in amazement to the boys' story. When it was finished, Mr. Hardy leaned forward intently in his chair and reached for the telephone.

"I think we have our man," he said, as he lifted the receiver and waited for the operator. "The light-colored scar on the chin is the give-away. The description fits an Indian by the name of Nanab. He is Rahmud Ghapur's personal servant!"

CHAPTER XX

A Nautical Clue

TEN minutes later Mr. Hardy replaced the instrument in its cradle and turned to them. "Well, boys, the pieces are beginning to fall into place. Ghapur says that his servant Nanab quit his job very suddenly the day before yesterday and has disappeared."

"Wow!" cried Joe, adding, "Why didn't Mr. Delhi recognize him while staying at Ghapur's home?"

"Nanab apparently kept out of his sight on purpose," Mr. Hardy replied. "He may have feared he might be recognized. The only relative in India that Nanab wrote to while he was in Washington," Mr. Hardy continued, "was a brother whose name is Bangalore. So far as Ghapur knows, Bangalore is still in India."

Frank broke in excitedly. "No, Dad. You were away when we learned this, but Bangalore was the name of an Indian who jumped ship on the *Continental* while the vessel was docked in New York. That happened two years ago."

As he finished speaking, Radley came in, an envelope in his hand. He said he had been to the house and was amazed to learn of the bombing and was glad the Hardys were safe. He now handed over the envelope, saying:

"I came down here to check my mail. When I opened this, I knew you boys would want to see it." He held up a photograph. "It's a picture of that fellow Bangalore. The steamship line sent it."

"Bangalore!" Mr. Hardy exclaimed. "He's Nanab's brother all right. Looks just like him, except that the chin scar's missing. Good work, fellows. It certainly looks as if Bangalore is one of the ringleaders in this smuggling and kidnaping business. Nanab has probably been working with him part of the time and is now spending full time on the rackets."

"Dad, do you think he could have been the one who intercepted Mr. Ghapur's letter to us?" Joe asked.

"No doubt of it. Unfortunately, Ghapur trusted Nanab implicitly and always confided in him. Nanab destroyed the letter, but why do you suppose he let the falcon come through to you?"

"That does seem strange," Frank agreed. "Anyway, we know he learned all the plans and developments in the case by eavesdropping on Ghapur and Mr. Delhi."

"There's one bright side to this whole thing," said his father. "You boys must be much nearer a solution than you think, or I doubt that Nanab would have left his job at Ghapur's. He probably knew the net was closing around him."

Frank and Joe, certain that part of the solution was to be found on the *Daisy K,* determined to carry through with their fishing plan. Since it was too late for the trip scheduled for that day, Frank phoned the booking office for Bayport's charter boats to find out if the *Daisy K* was going out the following morning. He was delighted to learn there would be a trip.

Mr. Hardy said he would make the necessary arrangements for repairs to their home, then he must return to Washington on urgent business.

The phone rang and Joe answered. The caller was Chet, who said, "How about you fellows coming out here to live until your house is repaired? The folks say it's fine with them."

"Sounds good, Chet. Wait till I ask Dad and Mother."

The family agreed that the brothers would enjoy staying with Chet far more than living in the hotel, so Joe promptly accepted. Then, at their parents' request, Frank and Joe worked nearly all day at the bombed house storing away pictures, lamps, and other small furnishings, and moving clothes to the hotel. It was late afternoon when they arrived at the Morton farm.

"Before it gets dark today," Frank proposed, "let's go over to the deserted hunting lodge and see if Radley has anything new to report."

After the Hardys had deposited their luggage in the Mortons' guest room, the three boys set off for the lodge. Radley said there was no evidence that anyone had returned to the lodge and felt further watch of it was useless. He remarked that he would like to tackle the mystery from another angle.

"I've had a lot of time to think out here," he said, "and just this morning I came up with an idea. Maybe these smugglers don't send their pigeons from a boat at all. They may be working from an island."

"An island! Maybe that's it!" Joe replied enthusiastically. "When we get back to Chet's, let's take a look at a map to see what's northeast of here."

"And," said Radley, "why not let me cut loose with a plane and see if I can spot something out there."

"Okay," Frank agreed. "Joe and I are planning a fishing trip on the *Daisy K* early tomorrow morning. Among the three of us we may uncover something either on the sea or from the air."

Radley and the boys walked back to the Morton home where they pored over a map.

"Hmm," said Radley. "Islands galore northeast of here. The closest ones are Shoals, Pine Haven, and Venus, but that doesn't mean they're the ones. The smugglers may be taking no chances and using an island quite a distance away. I'll look over as many as I can from the plane, though."

That evening, after Radley had left, Frank and Joe got their fishing disguises ready. Their father, an expert at disguise, had taught his sons many of the techniques. First came a make-up base: ruddy for Joe, slightly sallow for Frank. Then Frank pasted on a false chin stubble and sideburns, while Joe gummed on a small mustache and heavy false eyebrows, then plastered down his blond, slightly wavy hair. With slickers and sou'westers in case of rain, they looked like middle-aged fishermen. Iola and Chet laughed heartily at their disguises.

"Nobody will know you," Iola declared.

Before dawn the next morning, Frank and Joe repaired their make-up and set out through a drizzle for the wharf where the *Daisy K* was tied up. Four other sports fishermen already were there, ready to go aboard. The Hardys kept a wary eye on Captain Flont, who did not give any indication that he recognized them. In fact, he paid little attention to his passengers.

The day's fishing went along with reasonable success. All of the members of the *Daisy K*'s passenger list managed to net a fair-sized catch of tuna and mackerel. Under various reasonable pretexts during the trip, both Frank and Joe wandered all over the craft, but the falcon was not aboard. The boys had also made a point of trying to pick up conversations between the captain, his crew of two, and any passengers that might be in league with him, but learned nothing.

In the late afternoon, when the *Daisy K* started back for Bayport, Frank and Joe were seated inside the deckhouse as close as they dared to Captain Flont, who was at the wheel.

Suddenly, above the roar of the motors, they heard him say to one of his crew, "It beats me where Ragu went."

"I'm afraid he's in trouble," the man replied.

"It's going to be hard to take care of things at windward without him," the captain said, then shifted the conversation to another subject.

Frank gripped Joe's arm. At windward! His younger brother nodded.

The boys got up and walked out to the stern of the boat. When they were alone, Frank whispered, "Did you have the same thought I did? That it was strange for a nautical man to say '*at* windward'?"

"I sure did," Joe replied. "If he had meant a direction, the captain would have said 'to windward.' "

"*Right. Windward must be a place!*"

The *Daisy K* reached port just before suppertime. As Frank and Joe walked along the water front with their day's catch of fish, they questioned sailors from other boats about Windward. No one had heard of it. Finally they headed for the hotel, deciding to have supper with the family before going to Chet's.

The boys, still in their disguises, turned their mackerel over to a startled bellhop and asked him to deliver them to the hotel chef. Then, learning from the desk clerk that Radley was back, they went at once to his room. The detective grinned at their disguise. While they were removing the make-up, he said:

"I flew all over the coast for about five hours, but I couldn't spot any activity that would indicate smuggling operations. I did see several deserted sections along the shores of some of the islands that would make good hideaways. Guess we'll have to investigate all of them."

"Ever hear of a place called Windward?" Frank inquired.

"No," Radley replied. "What about it?"

The older boy repeated the conversation that he and Joe had overheard on the *Daisy K.* Radley nodded thoughtfully, then remarked:

"Let's go down to the Skippers Club. I know some of the old seafaring men who stay there. Maybe one of them will be able to help us out."

After supper with Mrs. Hardy and Aunt Gertrude, the three went to the old salt-box building near the water front, where many of the old-timers played cribbage, chess, and billiards in between spinning sea yarns about the good old days. Sam Radley was hailed by several of the captains. He quizzed some of them about Windward. The name meant nothing to the first half dozen he spoke to, but finally a grizzled man of the sea looked up from a game of solitaire.

"Sure, I know the place. Windward was our old-timers' name fer the windside o' Venus Island," he said. "The lee side's green and right purty. Folks live there. But Windward—it's rocky and barren. Broken up by stretches o' pine woods here and there."

Radley thanked the old salt and the three left the club. Outside, Frank remarked, "That sounds like an ideal spot for smuggling operations!"

"Yes," Radley replied.

"Let's check on it right away," Joe proposed. "Maybe we can round up some of the fellows to help us."

"As a matter of fact," said Frank, "Biff Hooper and Tony Prito were going out to Chet's tonight. Let's put all three of them to work on the case."

Radley was game and said he was eager to go along. They stopped at a drugstore with a couple of phone booths. Joe called Chet to explain their plan to take the *Sleuth* out to Venus Island for a reconnoitering expedition.

"Sounds like a dangerous job," said Chet, "but I'll come and bring Tony and Biff. I expect them here any minute."

"Meet us at our boathouse," Joe directed. "And make it as soon as you can."

Frank, meanwhile, had called the hotel from the other phone booth to apprise his mother of their plans. Next, he put in a call to Chief Collig, telling him of their new lead and asking if Ragu could be held for a day or two longer, without visitors if possible, while they tracked down the lead.

"Don't worry about that," the chief replied. "He's refused to see anyone, even an attorney! He's made no attempt to raise the bail money, either. Frank, that fellow is plenty scared of someone!"

"And," Frank said, "my guess would be it's Captain Flont!" Pleased with the news about Ragu, he said good-by and hung up. Then he headed for the boathouse with Radley and Joe. A quick look around showed that repairs were well under way and that the *Sleuth* could be returned to its berth before long.

Presently Chet's jalopy rattled up the street and pulled to a stop. Lanky, good-natured Biff Hooper swung his long legs over the side, and Tony Prito followed. Chet squeezed himself out of the driver's seat and joined the group.

They all walked to the *Sleuth* and went aboard. It was just past midnight as Frank took them across Barmet Bay, out through the inlet, and into the swells of the ocean beyond. They talked over their program.

"When we get to Windward, we'll cruise around and find out what we can," Frank said. "If we don't learn anything, then Joe and Radley and I will go ashore to investigate."

Tony, who owned a boat of his own, would be left in charge of the *Sleuth*.

Two hours later the forbidding rocky slopes of Windward were etched in black against the moon-lit sky. The motor of the *Sleuth* was throttled down and a search of the waters began. They found no boats anchored and none were visible in any of the many inlets among the rocks.

At three fifteen, Radley and the Hardys decided to go ashore. They donned their swimming trunks and slid over the side without a sound.

Treading water beside the boat, Frank said to the boys in the *Sleuth*, "You fellows cruise back and forth, keeping your eyes open for anything that might be stirring. We'll swim out again just at daybreak and meet you."

Chet, Tony, and Biff wished them luck, then started off. They cruised around for an hour without seeing another boat or sighting anything suspicious. Finally, as the first streak of light appeared in the east, Tony moved the *Sleuth* to the spot where they had left the swimmers.

After what seemed like a long wait, Tony said, "Fellows, I'm worried. Frank and Joe and Radley are overdue."

The three in the boat gazed across the water but could not see anyone along the shore or in the water that lay between the *Sleuth* and the rocky beach. Tony moved the boat a little closer and got out the binoculars. There was not a sign of anyone on the rocks.

"I'll—I'll bet the smugglers got 'em!" Chet said nervously. "What'll we do now?"

"Give 'em fifteen minutes," Tony advised, "and then storm that island!"

CHAPTER XXI

Forbidding Island

FRANK, Joe, and Radley had swum easily to the narrow, rocky beach on the windward side of Venus Island. The water was chilly, but their brisk strokes had kept them from feeling the cold.

A jagged cliff that rose abruptly about twenty feet back from the shore was clearly outlined in the moonlight. The swimmers, sure now that no guard was on watch on the beach, walked out of the surf and brushed the water from their bodies. In the warm night air they gazed around the desolate beach but could see no evidence of anyone having been there recently.

"But we couldn't be sure of finding any definite clues on the shore here," Frank mused. "Footprints or signs of beaching a boat could have been washed out by the waves."

They climbed a trail that wound up the face of the cliff and turned their attention to a woods of wind-swept pines, which came to within a hundred feet of the cliff's edge. The three sleuths peered ahead intently. Frank, first to spy a light among the trees, said:

"I wonder if that light is coming from a house in there? I thought this place was uninhabited."

"Let's find out," Joe urged.

They found a path that wound in and out among the trees and followed it until Joe held up his hand in warning.

"I think I hear voices!"

He and the others paused to listen. Not far from them several men were talking, part of the time in English, part in a foreign tongue the trio had come to recognize as a dialect of India.

The Hardys and Radley settled down behind a clump of bushes, trying to fathom the conversation which went on for some time. The voices carried clearly on the night air, and the listeners were provoked at not being able to translate the alien words. Presently, however, the sleuths were electrified upon hearing:

"Cap's late. I hope he didn't run into trouble. A motorboat was cruising around here a while ago. Better go take a look."

There was no oral response to the command, but a blond man began to walk toward the sleuths, who dodged out of his sight just in time. After he had gone a short distance, they followed silently, hoping the *Sleuth* was now far enough from the island not to be noticed.

"If that fellow has a boat hidden nearby and tries to set out for the *Sleuth*," Joe whispered tensely, "we'll jump him!"

"You bet!" Frank replied.

The man paused briefly at the edge of the cliff, then gingerly made his way down the trail to the beach. Radley and the Hardys crept to the brink and peered below. They did not see the *Sleuth*, but a surprise awaited them. A large motor dory, its engine off, was being propelled by oars toward the beach. As they watched, it glided to a stop just beyond the rocky shore. The watchers could see two men in the dory, but the figures were not close enough to be identified.

"Say, Frank," Joe whispered, "that sure looks like the same dory that met the *Daisy K* the night of the moonlight ride."

The blond man on the stony shore gave a low whistle. Almost instantly Radley and the boys became aware of tramping feet and a few moments later a dozen dark-skinned men, carrying trousers and shoes, came down the trail, passing just a few feet from the intruders. They were followed by a second light-haired man. When they reached the beach, this man pointed to the dory and immediately the dark-skinned men splashed through the waves toward it.

"Smuggled Indians!" Joe said in a hoarse whisper. "Let's try to stop them!"

Radley gripped the boy's arm. "That would only mean our capture. They outnumber us almost six to one!"

Joe calmed down as the aliens climbed aboard and the oars dipped into the surf. The dory was some distance from shore before the engine was started up.

As the two islanders came up the path and moved off among the trees, Frank suddenly gripped Joe's arm.

"Those men are obviously guards here," he said. "Do you suppose they're the two we watched being transferred from the *Daisy K* to the motor dory?"

Suddenly Joe sprang into action, and without a sound set off on a run among the trees after the blond men.

"Come on!" he called in a hoarse whisper. "Let's collar them."

Frank and Radley tried to stop Joe, because they felt there might be more than two in the island gang. If the Hardys and Radley were captured, any chance of further spying was out of the question!

Frank and the operative hurried after Joe, but within a few seconds, sounds of a struggle reached their ears.

"This means trouble," Frank whispered grimly.

Silently they rushed along the path and a few minutes later spotted the two guards and their prisoner approaching a group of small buildings set deep in a grove and almost hidden from view. One of the men kicked open the door of the nearest building and Joe was thrust into a lighted room.

"We've got to free him!" Frank said. "I don't care about the risk. This gang will stop at nothing!"

Radley restrained him. "Hold it, Frank," he said sternly. "Brute force isn't the answer. Look what just happened to Joe. The thing to do is to outwit these men."

"You're right, of course," Frank replied. "Tell you what," he said, noticing that the sky was lightening. "Tony, Chet, and Biff will be waiting offshore. Suppose you swim out to the *Sleuth* and try to follow the dory with the aliens in it. See where it goes. Then bring help back here. In the meantime, I'll try to think up a way to free Joe and maybe pick up more evidence."

His companion nodded and left at once. Frank waited until he heard the familiar roar of the *Sleuth's* engine as it took off at high speed, before he started his own work. Moving swiftly and cautiously, he edged in close to Joe's prison.

Through a closed window in the side of the cabin, he saw, to his dismay, that his brother had been bound to a chair. A coil of rope and a knife lay on a nearby table.

As he watched helplessly, the two middle-aged guards began cuffing Joe's face. Quickly Frank moved to another window which was open. He heard one of the guards say:

"This kid just won't talk. Put the gag back in."

"You can't convince me," the other man said as he replaced the gag, "that he came to Windward to swim all by himself in the middle of the night. He's a spy. We ought to check the area to see if there are any pals of his lurking around."

Frank ducked around the corner just in time. For, at that moment, the door of the cabin burst open and the two men rushed out. Frank, desperately realizing he must conceal himself, dodged behind a tree.

One of the guards announced he would circle the cabin. Frank held his breath, but the man passed without noticing him. The other zigzagged through the woods between the house and the beach, looking for trespassers, but shortly returned to report there was no evidence of other intruders.

The two men re-entered the house, but took up positions in such a way that Frank could not possibly move in on them without being seen.

A few minutes later one of the guards said, "Keep an eye on our prisoner while I eat breakfast. I'll spell you later, after I've talked to Cap. I've got a hunch about this kid!"

Frank wondered what he meant, then smiled triumphantly. This was his chance to free Joe!

He ducked into hiding again as the guard came out, closed the door carefully behind him, and walked toward one of the other buildings. Frank waited until the man had entered the cabin, which stood about a hundred yards away, then quietly moved to the door of Joe's prison and slowly turned the knob. The door was unlocked!

Picking up a piece of shale from the path, Frank flipped it at a windowpane. As the piece of rock crashed through, Joe's guard whirled away from the boy's side and dashed to the window. At the same time, Frank flattened himself against the door, his hand on the knob. As the guard gingerly leaned out the shattered window, Frank eased open the door and silently entered the room, his bare feet making no sound.

Joe was so relieved to see Frank he might have given his brother's presence away if he had not been gagged. With lightning speed, Frank whipped the gag from Joe's mouth with one hand, and with the other hand grabbed the knife from the table and slashed at the rope which bound Joe's hands together.

This was barely accomplished when the man at the window pulled his head in and started to turn around. Before he could see what was going on behind him, Frank gripped the man around the throat, stuffed the gag in his mouth, and caught one of his arms in a judo hold. Frank threw him to the floor, and Joe, now free, bound the guard with the rope that had seconds before secured him.

Their prisoner glared at the brothers as they consulted in low tones. "I sure messed this deal up," Joe remarked ruefully. "Thanks for turning the tables."

Frank grinned understandingly and said they must hurry or both of them might be caught. "I'll keep a lookout in this room while you investigate the rest of the cabin," he said.

Joe picked up a flashlight from the table in order to explore the dark rooms beyond. Frank posted himself at the door. In twenty seconds Joe was back at his brother's side.

"There are two more rooms in this building," Joe reported. "One's locked and—what do you know?—in the other there are five carrier pigeons in cages!"

Frank was excited at this news. "That clinches it. We've come to the right place. Let's go see if we can find out if Cap is who I think he is."

The boys checked the bonds on their prisoner, then rolled him under one of the bunks which lined two walls, and left the cabin. As they approached the building which the other guard had entered, Frank pointed out a high radio aerial that rose from the roof. "That's a powerful set," he said.

They peered cautiously in a window, and noted that it must be the building where the guards and aliens ate their meals. At one end was an old-fashioned cooking stove. Two long dining tables, capable of seating a large number of people, filled the other side of the big room.

Seated at a smaller table which stood against the far wall was the guard. In front of him was a short-wave sending and receiving radio. Over it, he was sending the startling announcement:

Joe sent the man sprawling away from the
short-wave radio.

"We've captured a spy. From your description, I think it's one of those Hardy boys!"

Frank and Joe gulped. The news was out! But no more must be sent!

Joe sprang through the doorway and threw himself at the man, knocking him away from the instrument and clipping him soundly on the jaw. The man sprawled on the floor, unconscious.

With the signal button released, the sending set was cut off. Frank, who had followed his brother into the room, instantly turned on the receiver. The cold, hard voice of Captain Flont was saying:

"I think we're being followed! But I can't afford any trouble! I'm going to open fire!"

Terror in their eyes, Frank's and Joe's hearts sank.

"The *Sleuth!*" both boys thought. "It must be the *Sleuth* that Captain Flont has spotted!"

CHAPTER XXII

An Escaped Prisoner

A FEELING of utter hopelessness swept over both Hardy boys. They realized that there was no way to reach the *Sleuth* and warn their friends that Captain Flont intended to fire on them!

Frank paced up and down the cabin, clenching his fists. Then, suddenly, he thought of a way in which Captain Flont might be tricked into changing his mind.

Grabbing a paper napkin from one of the dining tables, Frank wrapped it around the mouthpiece of the short-wave sender. Perhaps the napkin would serve to muffle his voice enough to prevent its being recognized when he sent a message. He cleared his throat, pressed the sending button, and said:

"Flont! Don't shoot! Orders from the boss!"

Frank clicked on the receiver but there was no answer. He kept repeating "Come in, Flont." Still no reply. As Joe looked on tensely, Frank continued this call intermittently for ten minutes. Finally, receiving no response from the captain, he gave up.

"Maybe Flont had turned off his set before I started sending my order," Frank said, worried. "Or he may have recognized my voice."

"You tried the only thing possible, Frank. It was a clever trick, too!" Joe assured his brother loyally. "Besides, even if there wasn't any answer, Flont might have heard it and been fooled. All we can do is hope he obeys."

Joe suggested that he hurry across to the other side of the island and contact the local police. "In the meantime, you stand by the radio, just in case Flont should call in again."

"Okay," Frank agreed. "But let's tie this fellow up first. He's coming to and we don't want any more trouble."

Using heavy twine, they bound the captive's ankles and arms securely, and put a gag in his mouth. Joe found a pair of shoes and a sweater, put them on, and started off.

He located a rocky trail that seemed to lead toward the inhabited part of the island and followed it a couple of miles, until he came out of the woods. Finally, nearly an hour after leaving the smugglers' hut, Joe spotted a farmhouse and dashed up to it.

Fortunately, the residents were awake. They listened in amazement and with some skepticism to the boy's story. But they permitted Joe to use their phone and offered to drive him to the chief of police in Venus Village.

Joe tried unsuccessfully to call one number after another on the mainland. He could not get through to either Chief Collig or his mother at the Bayport Hotel, due to the inadequate service between the island and Bayport. After several attempts, however, he finally contacted the Coast Guard. The young detective was told that men would be sent out at once to apprehend Captain Flont and learn what had happened to Chet and the others on the *Sleuth*.

On the drive to town the farmer remarked, "This is the first time I remember anything happening around here which needed the police. Chief Barton's appointment was kind of an honorary one."

When the farmer stopped at the police chief's home in Venus Village, Joe thanked him for the lift, then rang the bell.

Chief Barton himself opened the door. He was a man past middle age, with a paunch and a good-natured smile.

"Well, what brings you around here so early in the morning, stranger?" the man asked, suppressing a yawn.

"I'm Joe Hardy from Bayport. My brother and I have located the hide-out of a ring of smugglers here on Venus Island. It's on the windward side. We've got two of them tied up. We'd like you to come and make the arrests."

"Smugglers on Venus Island!" The chief blinked, then roared with laughter. "Who you trying to kid, son?"

"I tell you, sir, it's true," Joe insisted, trying not to show the annoyance he felt at the man's reaction. "The Coast Guard and the Immigration Service have been trying to track them down for months. The State Department's interested, too!"

"How does the State Department figure in this?" the officer asked curiously.

"These smugglers are also kidnapers," Joe explained. "They're holding an Indian prince captive —and are demanding one ransom payment after another."

"Indian! That's rich!" the chief guffawed. "Is he Sioux or Blackfoot?"

"He's a native of India, not an American Indian," Joe told him sharply, "and this is no laughing matter."

The man finally seemed to realize the seriousness of the situation and said, "Well, there ain't no one can say that Chief Barton don't tend to business when it comes his way. I'll phone my deputy and we'll be right with you. Jest sit down in the parlor and wait."

It seemed an eternity to Joe while Chief Barton made the contact with his deputy and dressed. But at last the chief brought in a tall, lanky man whom he introduced as Al Richards. The deputy, a quizzical expression on his face, studied Joe for a moment, then commented:

"So you're one of them Hardy boys, eh? I've heard tell about all the trouble you fellows get mixed up in down around Bayport. What's this wild-goose chase we're going on now?"

"Smugglers!" Joe said tersely. "And let's get going before it's too late."

The young sleuth had no intention of arguing with these men now that he had at least aroused their interest. The three drove part way back to the smugglers' hide-out in a jeep, apparently the only vehicle Venus Village possessed in the way of a police patrol car. They pulled to a stop about a mile from the cabins, and Joe led the men the rest of the way on foot. A fork in the path brought them to the cabin where Joe had been a prisoner.

Frank, who had found shoes and a shirt to fit him, heard them coming and went to meet the group. He said he certainly was glad to see the police officers and reported that no radio messages had been received.

"One of the smugglers is in here," he told the men, as they paused at the cabin door.

"Well," drawled Deputy Richards, "we're ready for him. Let's see what a smuggler looks like."

They opened the door and Joe walked across to the bunk. He knelt down to pull out the trussed-up figure.

He was not there!

"Our prisoner's gone!" Joe cried, unable to believe his eyes.

"Gone!" echoed Frank. "But how?"

Deputy Richards looked at his chief and remarked

laconically, "Told you this would be a wild-goose chase!"

For answer, the chief shook his head slowly and shrugged, eying Frank and Joe dubiously. The Hardys, however, were not looking at the chief. They were staring at each other, blaming themselves for the prisoner's getaway. Apparently they had not tied him securely enough.

But perhaps he had not had time to go far, the boys thought. In fact, he might still be in the building! To satisfy their curiosity, they dashed into the adjoining room. The escaped man was not there and only three of the pigeons were left in the cages.

Frank tried the door to the next room—the one Joe had reported locked. It was unlocked now.

As the door swung open a strange and wholly unexpected scene met their eyes. Joe cried out, "Here he is!" and Frank yelled, "Stop!"

The police chief and his deputy rushed in. At a window the man who had been the Hardys' prisoner was just releasing two carrier pigeons.

Joe, noticing there were capsules on the birds' legs, leaped forward, trying to stop their flight. But he was too late!

"Where were those messages going?" he demanded, but the man made no reply.

Suddenly Frank saw a large perch in a corner. On it rested a hooded hawk. Certain that the falcon was their own, he picked up a heavy leather gauntlet from a window sill. Quickly donning the glove,

Frank took the bird on his wrist. As he removed the hood, Frank spoke softly to her. The hawk recognized him instantly and uttered a joyful *keer, keer.* He stroked her a few times, then hooded her again.

Frank turned to the officers and said, "Here is support for our story. This is a prize hunting hawk, and it was stolen from our home in Bayport."

"Arrest this man!" Joe said. "He's in cahoots with the thief and he's one of the smugglers."

But Chief Barton made no move to take the man into custody. Instead, he blinked at the smuggler. "Why, John Cullen, what's going on?" he asked. "What're you doin' here?"

Frank was puzzled by the chief's friendliness, but he did not take time to ask questions. He was afraid that the pigeons might be carrying notes which would alert the men holding the prince. If so, there was no telling what harm might come to the Indian youth. Frank hurried outdoors with the falcon and unhooded her.

Looking up, he saw that the carrier pigeons were circling above the cabin, picking up their directional beam preparatory to making a beeline flight to their destination. There was not a second to lose!

Frank turned the falcon loose and murmured softly, "Get one, old girl! Get both, if you can!"

To Frank's dismay, the falcon responded sluggishly. Her reactions were considerably slowed down as a result of being imprisoned for so long. There was nothing the impatient young detective could do to hasten matters, however. He must wait until she regained her keenness.

At that moment Chief Barton and Deputy Richards came out of the cabin with John Cullen and Joe. In an angry tone the chief of police said to the boys:

"If your whole story's as phony as this part of it, I'm afraid we can't help you."

"What do you mean by that?" Joe demanded.

"This so-called smuggler, Mr. Cullen, is one of the leading citizens here on the island, though he has only lived here a couple of years. He's a pigeon fancier and has been racing birds for a year or more. His cote's on the mainland."

The Hardys were not impressed. Turning to Cullen, Joe asked suspiciously:

"How do you account for our stolen falcon being in your cabin?"

"My assistant got overenthusiastic about the whole deal, I'm afraid," the man replied suavely.

"What do you mean?" Joe probed.

"He knew that a number of my best pigeons had been killed by a hunting hawk. Someone told him that your falcon was responsible."

Frank's and Joe's minds were racing. Surely none of their friends, including Ahmed, who knew the secret, would have given it away. Suddenly a thought came to them. *Nanab!* He had doubtless brought the falcon to the island!

"Go on!" Frank said icily to Cullen.

"My assistant brought the bird here, so that I could use it as evidence in my damage suit against you," the man concluded triumphantly.

It was obvious that both Chief Barton and Deputy Richards believed the story and were about to reproach the boys when Joe challenged Cullen with:

"That sounds smooth enough. Now try to explain why the other man we captured was talking by short wave to a boat with smuggled aliens in it."

"You're crazy," Cullen retorted. "Chief Barton, these boys are the ones who ought to be arrested!"

All this time Frank had not taken his eyes off the falcon. She had finally aroused from her lethargy and was now winging after the two pigeons. The hawk was still some distance from the birds, who were lining out for the mainland. Completely confident of the falcon's skill, Frank remarked:

"Chief Barton, maybe our hunting hawk will prove to you that Mr. Cullen is not merely racing pigeons. *She* may prove he is aiding smugglers and kidnapers!"

All eyes turned toward the three birds in the morning sky. The falcon was making wide circles that carried her ever higher. Her deep, purposeful wing beats seemed slow to the anxious boys, but they noticed that she was rapidly outclimbing the pigeons!

CHAPTER XXIII

The Falcon's Victory

THE falcon was now only a tiny speck in the sky. The pigeons were out over the water but well below the climbing hawk. Frank turned to Joe and said:

"I guess this is what those old-time falconers called a 'ringing flight.' I'm going to the beach to watch it." The others followed him.

At the height of her pitch the falcon plunged toward the pigeons in a long, angling stoop. Faster and faster she dropped—until the onlookers saw only a blur of moving wings. At a speed approaching a hundred and eighty miles an hour the hawk struck one of the pigeons. It plummeted into the water.

The peregrine mounted from her stoop and gave chase to the remaining pigeon.

Frank shouted, "Joe, take this and watch Cullen!" He thrust the hawk's hood into Joe's hand and ran into the surf. He set off at a strong, fast crawl toward the floating pigeon and soon reached it.

As Frank swam back to the beach with it, he glanced up. The second pigeon had reversed its course and was heading toward the brushy cover of the island. With awe and admiration he and Joe watched their falcon overtake her prey in a tail chase and bind to it in mid-air. In a long glide Miss Peregrine came to rest with her quarry in her talons.

"Good girl!" Joe cried. He ran forward and picked up the pigeon.

At that moment Frank came out of the surf and joined Joe. John Cullen cried angrily, "Leave those birds alone! They're my property!" With a vicious lunge he grabbed for both of them.

To the boys' dismay, Chief Barton said, "I guess he's right, fellows. Let him have them."

Frank and Joe were nonplused. "I'll give them to you, Chief, but not to this man," Frank said firmly.

As he spoke, Frank flipped off the capsule from the leg of the pigeon he was holding, while Joe removed the one on the other bird. Cullen tried to snatch the capsules, screaming in a hysterical, high-pitched voice that this was thievery and against the law. He demanded that the policemen do something.

But the chief and his deputy seemed paralyzed by the swift-moving events. Before the men could collect their wits, the Hardys had twisted open the tops of the capsules.

Into Frank's hand dropped two rubies!

Joe's capsule contained a tightly folded note which he opened and read aloud:

" '12 A's gone. Spies here. We're leaving island. Advise you move at once.' "

Chief Barton stared in amazement. Turning to Cullen, he demanded, "What does this mean?"

But Cullen was already fleeing pell-mell over the rocks.

"I guess that proves he's guilty!" Joe exclaimed. "12 A's must mean those aliens who left here in the dory!"

Stuffing the note into his pocket, he dashed after Cullen, with the police at his heels. The chase was soon over. As the fugitive attempted to get away in a motorboat hidden in a cove, he was caught and marched back.

"I guess you're not innocent after all," said Chief Barton. "But you sure had me fooled."

Cullen's jaw was grimly set and he looked with hatred at the Hardys. "You idiots!" he stormed. "I'll get you for this!"

Frank suggested to the police officers that they pick up the other prisoner at once. Silently he and Joe hoped this man had not been able to loosen his bonds and send a message!

Frank hooded the falcon and led the way to the second cabin. They found the man on the floor, still bound and gagged. Chief Barton stared at him, then exclaimed in amazement:

"Arthur Daly! You mixed up with the smugglers, too!" He turned to the boys and remarked, "Mr.

Daly owns one of our most successful lobster businesses."

The Hardys did not comment on this revelation, but Frank said, "I suggest you handcuff these men to avoid any further trouble."

At a gesture from Barton, Deputy Richards took care of this detail. Then the chief posed importantly before his prisoners and barked:

"Now let's hear the truth about this whole thing!"

The men refused to talk, but the Hardys explained what they knew of the illicit entries of the Indians, the kidnaping of Prince Tava, and the ransom demanded in rubies.

"The pigeons carried the rubies and notes from here to their home cote," said Joe. "And that's the next place we'll have to locate."

The prisoners exchanged alarmed glances.

"Well, I swan!" Chief Barton cried. Addressing his deputy, he said ruefully, "With all this going on at Windward, I reckon we ought to turn in our badges."

"Maybe you won't have to," Frank told them. "If you'll take these men to jail and notify the Federal authorities, you'll be doing a good job."

Chief Barton suggested that they all proceed to town at once. Carrying the falcon and the three remaining pigeons, the group headed for the jeep. Barton promised to station men at Windward to take care of any smugglers who might show up.

Back at Venus Village, the once-respected islanders were put in cells, then Barton dispatched special deputies to the Windward area. Next, he talked by phone to the Immigration authorities. Ten minutes later, a broad smile on his face, he leaned back in his chair and said:

"Things are moving along fine. The Federal men will be out soon to take over. They'll get any more aliens or ransom being brought here."

"Good," said Joe. "And now may I phone the Coast Guard? I want to find out what happened to the friends who came out here with us."

"Go ahead," the chief replied.

At the first words of Lieutenant Commander Wilson, who answered, Joe let out a whistle, and turning his head, he said in an aside to Frank, "They caught Flont and his two crewmen as well as those twelve smuggled aliens! They're at the Coast Guard station now."

As Joe listened intently to the lieutenant commander he sobered. Putting down the phone, he reported that there was no news of their friends. Flont would not say whether he had fired on them before his capture. A Coast Guard helicopter was out now searching for the *Sleuth*.

The Hardys were greatly worried about their friends. Frank asked, "Chief, could someone take us back to the mainland right away?"

"Sure thing," Barton agreed. "I'll run you to Bayport myself in my own motorboat. And say, will you fellows take these pigeons? I don't know what to do with 'em and you might find the birds useful."

"Okay. We will," said Frank.

Chief Barton kept his boat in good shape, and a little over an hour later, the chief, Frank and Joe, the hooded hawk and the three pigeons were speeding across Barmet Bay toward Bayport. Suddenly, Joe, who had been scanning the water through binoculars, called:

"There's the *Sleuth* now, Frank! And all our friends are aboard!"

About a quarter of a mile ahead was the Hardys' boat. Barton sounded his siren and minutes later he drew alongside the *Sleuth*.

"You all right?" everyone asked simultaneously.

Upon being assured that all were unharmed, Frank introduced the police captain. Then Chet, his eyes bulging, said, "You got the falcon back! And are those the smugglers' pigeons?"

"They sure are," Chief Barton replied. "And we got the ringleaders behind bars, too!"

Frank and Joe let this remark go unchallenged, although they knew the hardest part of the case—catching the real ringleaders—still faced them. They told their friends that Captain Flont had been captured, then asked what had happened to the group in the *Sleuth*.

"We g-got fired on," Chet answered promptly. "The captain missed, thank goodness, and he didn't try again. I don't know why."

"Because Frank short-waved him not to," Joe said, and explained about the radio message. "Then what happened?"

Tony, Chet, and Biff tried to tell the story at the same time. At last Radley summarized the situation.

"We picked up the trail of the *Daisy K* shortly after I swam back to the *Sleuth*. Captain Flont had already picked up the smuggled Indians from the motor dory. What we didn't know was that Flont had a long-range rifle and we were his target! I think Flont fired the first shot to scare us, because I don't see how he could have missed!

"Before he could follow it up with another, Frank's message must have reached him. Anyway, he stopped firing and started off, full speed ahead. When we followed, he kept the rifle trained on us. We finally gave up the chase, deciding to make a wide sweep around him, then race to shore and send the Coast Guard out for the *Daisy K*."

Radley went on to say that as they headed for a cove, the *Sleuth* suddenly ran out of gas. "And to make matters worse," he continued with a wry smile, "the emergency fuel can was empty."

The operative said that another boat had finally come by. As it was transferring fuel, the Coast Guard helicopter flew over, hovered just above them, and dropped a note instructing them to proceed to Bayport.

When Frank and Joe finished comparing notes with their friends on the night's adventures, the

Hardys climbed into their own boat, taking the birds with them. The police chief promised to keep the Hardys informed of island developments and added, "Thanks again for saving my job regarding those smugglers!"

As soon as they reached Bayport, Radley and the Hardys headed for the Coast Guard station. There they discovered that Lieutenant Commander Wilson was questioning the prisoners himself. He had been in touch with Washington, and was impressed with the importance of the capture. He looked up as Frank, Joe, and Radley came in and beckoned them toward empty chairs alongside his desk.

Captain Flont winced at seeing Radley and glared at the Hardys as he was asked to repeat his statement.

"I've told you a dozen times I'm innocent," he declared. "I didn't know those Indians were aliens. Someone radioed to me that a party of picnickers had been stranded on Venus Island. They offered to pay me my usual fishing fee to bring them back to Bayport."

The lieutenant commander asked Frank, Joe, and Radley if they would like to question the captain.

Radley began. "Why did you fire on the *Sleuth?*"

Flont was ready with an answer. "You were following us, and it made my passengers nervous. I just fired in the air to scare you."

Frank walked over to the group of aliens and asked if any of them spoke English. One young man came forward. Smiling at him, Frank said:

"We are friends of Rahmud Ghapur and of Prince Bhagnav, cousin of the Maharajah of Hatavab. We'll be glad to help you if you will tell us the truth."

Flont's face turned purple with anger as he shouted, "You men shut up!"

The Indian talked with the other aliens for some time, then he turned back to Frank. "We sorry we break your law. We mean no harm. We pay these men lot of money for bring us to this country. Now bad trouble. We want to go home!"

Frank turned to the lieutenant commander and said, "I guess you've got your evidence."

"One more question," said Joe, looking at the young Indian. "While you were with these men who were trying to smuggle you in, did you ever hear anything about the kidnaping of Prince Tava?"

The spokesman shook his head violently. "Know nothing. Prince Tava kidnap, you say? What bad men do this?"

Joe did not answer the question. The Coast Guard officer thanked the Hardys and Radley for their help, then the three departed. The operative decided to return to Windward. He would wait for the Federal authorities and give them all available information on the case.

The boys went to the Bayport Hotel and immediately got in touch with their father in Washington. He was delighted with the turn the case had taken, and promised to fly home at once. He would ask Mr.

Delhi, who had arrived from New York the day before, to accompany him. Working together, the detective said, they ought to be able to locate the missing prince and wind up the case.

When the call was completed, Frank said, "Joe, I have a hunch we can have the mainland hide-out located by the time Dad and Mr. Delhi get here."

"How?"

Frank indicated the three cages with the pigeons in them. "We'll turn these birds loose from three different parts of the surrounding countryside and keep an eye on them with our glasses. If we map their lines of flight, they'll serve as bases for a triangulation fix."

"That's a swell idea," Joe agreed, "but first let's have lunch. I'm starved."

Immediately after a hearty meal, the boys began their work. Joe found a piece of paper, similar to those on which the other messages had been written, and printed:

"Sit tight. Everything okay this end."

He folded the message and inserted it in one of the capsules they had collected.

Meanwhile, Frank had hurried to see their jeweler friend. Mr. Bickford supplied him with four small imitation rubies that would lull the suspicions of the prince's kidnapers until the showdown.

When Frank returned, the brothers went to the roof of the hotel. From there they released the first pigeon with the message capsule. The Hardys watched the bird circle, then they lined up its course with a compass and marked the exact direction.

The boys divided the rubies between the two remaining pigeons. Joe took one bird five miles north of Bayport while Frank went five miles south with the other. When the brothers returned to the hotel they compared notes and marked the chart again. They grinned in satisfaction as they looked at the spot where the three lines crossed.

"I guess we've pinpointed the hide-out," said Frank. "It's at the top of Lion Mountain."

The almost inaccessible spot was about twenty-five miles from Bayport, and it was reputed that mountain lions once had inhabited it. A few years ago the boys had climbed to the top and knew that it was a rugged hike.

"Frank," Joe said, "I think you and I should investigate Lion Mountain at once."

"You mean not wait for Dad?"

"We don't dare wait, Frank. If Bangalore and Nanab learn that Flont has been captured, and realize their whole plot is falling apart, I'm afraid they'll take revenge on the prince!"

"You mean kill him?"

"Yes."

Frank weighed this suggestion a few moments, then nodded. "We'll go at once."

CHAPTER XXIV

Confessions

THE boys told their mother of the proposed plan and gave her the pinpointed map for Mr. Hardy. She said she would agree to their going only on one condition. They were to do nothing more than try to get word to Prince Tava and help him to escape.

"Leave the capture of those smugglers and kidnapers to your father and the police," she said, and Frank and Joe promised they would.

As the boys were about to depart, a telephone call came in from Radley, who said that the two men who ran the dory had been captured while docking it at Daly's lobster pound.

"Well, that settles everything from this end of the case," the operative said. "I'll be back shortly."

The boys told him their plan, and he wished them luck. When they arrived at the near side of Lion Mountain, Frank parked the convertible where it would not be spotted and they started off on foot.

"I wonder how near the top the hide-out is,"

Frank remarked. "Think we'd better circle the mountain to see if we can pick up a clue?"

"Yes. But I'll bet it's near the summit," said Joe.

"On the other hand," Frank said with a smile, "they might want to be nearer the bottom to get away in a hurry."

The brothers had nearly completed the circle before they found a clue. It was an indistinct trail and at once they began to follow it upward.

Frank and Joe proceeded cautiously, constantly on the lookout for any traps. Half a mile up the trail, Frank spotted a suspicious-looking pile of leaves and twigs in the path. Picking up a long stick, he gently poked at the leaves and in a few seconds uncovered a bear trap.

"Wow!" Joe said softly, as Frank threw a stone at it, springing the trap. "Did the smugglers or some trapper set that?"

Frank thought that probably the smugglers had. Farther on, they came across an uprooted tree cleverly braced into position, with its roots and a taut rope stretched across the trail, covered with dirt and leaves. But it was ready to fall on anyone who might happen to trip over the rope.

About half a mile from the top in an open section, the boys came to a barbed-wire fence. It was about eight feet high and the upper strands were tilted outward, making it almost impossible to scale.

"Look!" whispered Joe from the shelter of the trees. "That fence is electrified!"

"And probably has a charge heavy enough to knock a fellow out," Frank remarked. "I'll bet it sets off an alarm, too."

"What a way to be stymied," said Joe. "Just when we're ready to break the case."

Frank looked through the fence, his eyes probing the trees beyond. No one was in sight.

"What say we pole-vault over, Joe? Eight feet isn't too high."

"We'll do it," Joe said enthusiastically. "About a hundred yards back I saw some saplings that had blown down. We can use them."

He located two stout saplings which suited their purpose. One he tossed over the fence to use when coming back. Meanwhile, Frank had dug a heel hole just short of the fence and braced it with flat stones.

"I'll go first," said Joe.

"For Pete's sake, be careful," Frank warned. "Don't hit that fence!"

Joe ran forward lightly, hit the heel hole with a slight thud, and whipped up and over the fence. Frank grabbed the pole to keep it from striking the barrier.

Now Frank used the pole to vault over. His jump was a bit trickier than Joe's, because at the height of it he had to thrust back on the pole to keep it from hitting the fence and sounding an alarm.

Once inside, the Hardys knew the hardest part of their job lay ahead. Through the scrubby bushes and trees they could see several crudely constructed huts.

Near one of them stood a handsome, pensive-looking youth about eighteen years of age. He was holding a hooded goshawk. From the color of his skin and his characteristic features the Hardys were sure he was an Indian.

The boy must be Prince Tava!

Some distance from the prince the boys spotted several dark-skinned men. They were no doubt some of the smuggled Indians.

In the shelter of the trees, the Hardys crawled toward the prince. When they were close enough to talk to him without betraying themselves to the others, Frank called in a whisper:

"Prince!"

As the young man turned and stared, Frank smiled and went on quickly, "We are American friends sent here by your cousin Bhagnav."

The prince moved slowly toward the boys and asked in a low voice, "Why does Bhagnav send you here?"

"To rescue you from your kidnapers."

"But I was not kidnaped," the prince explained in some surprise. "The police are after me, and my friends are protecting me."

"That's not true," Frank insisted. "Your father has already paid a fabulous ransom in rubies for your return, but these people continue to hold you and demand more payment."

Prince Tava still did not seem to be convinced. The Hardys were trying hard to think of some way

Quickly he vaulted the electrified fence.

they could assure him of their sincerity. Finally Frank said:

"Your good friend Rahmud Ghapur is very much worried. He has engaged my father and brother and me to search for you. Mr. Ghapur told us of the time when he saved you in the cheetah hunt. He's afraid that you're in much greater danger now."

The prince's eyes widened. He whispered the name of Ghapur several times. Then he replied:

"If Rahmud Ghapur has sent you, then I will go with you."

"Act as if you were just strolling around and follow us," Frank directed.

The Hardys crawled away. The prince followed slowly, laughing and talking to the goshawk all the while. He acted as though he did not have a care in the world. When the three were well out of sight of the buildings, and close to the electrified fence, Joe said:

"I'm afraid you'll have to leave the goshawk here for now. Once we're out of this place and your abductors learn of your disappearance, they'll probably make trouble. We may become separated. If this happens, take our car and meet us at the Bayport Hotel. My mother and aunt are staying there. Ask for them." He added detailed instructions about the location of their hidden car and directions for reaching the hotel.

Prince Tava regretfully fastened his goshawk's leash to a tree, picked up the pole, and gracefully vaulted the fence. He moved off quickly into the shadows of the trees beyond. Joe, pole in hand, was getting set to make his jump when Frank heard someone running toward them from the rear.

"Jump, Joe!" Frank whispered fiercely. The next second, a lariat slapped over his shoulders.

As he hit the ground, Frank caught a glimpse of his brother, back arched, halfway up in his leap. But suddenly Joe was snatched violently from mid-air. Frank, his heart sinking, knew Joe had been lassoed, too.

A half-dozen fiery-eyed men gripped both boys roughly and dragged them toward one of the buildings. They were thrust through the doorway into a well-furnished room, and confronted by two handsome young Indians who resembled each other strongly. One, however, bore a light-colored scar on his chin.

Bangalore and Nanab!

"The Hardy boys!" Nanab gloated. "A fine catch indeed."

"What were you trying to accomplish here?" Bangalore demanded.

Joe tried to act casual and replied, "We came to get details of your smuggling and kidnaping plot. But I don't suppose that now we'll find out."

Nanab smiled, winked at Bangalore, and said, "Why not? We're proud of what we've done. We've fooled your authorities for a long time. Except for you two blundering boys, everything has run smoothly. Now that you are prisoners, we can tell you the full story, then arrange a convenient accident for you."

Bangalore gave his consent and Nanab began his story. "Captain Flont and his crew used the *Daisy K* to smuggle aliens into Bayport."

So Ragu had been lying all the time!

"Captain Flont," Bangalore went on, "is a clever man and will not betray us."

Despite the gravity of the situation, the Hardys could hardly keep from smiling. It was plain these ringleaders were not aware of the various arrests that had been made. Frank's message sent by the pigeon must have arrived. Now, if the Hardys could only keep these men talking long enough, Mr. Hardy and the police would have time to get there.

"We started making plans two years ago when Bangalore came to America," Nanab went on. "We spread word to dissatisfied citizens of our country that legal entry into the United States was impossible. However, by paying us a large fee they could be brought in surreptitiously and protected by us."

"How could you protect them?" Frank asked.

"We got them jobs and arranged for their social activities," Nanab explained.

"The kidnaping of the prince was my idea," Bangalore declared. "Both rackets were worked with Windward as the relay station. The property was bought cheap by two American friends of ours, John

Cullen and Arthur Daly. They fed and housed the aliens who came in on a special American–Far East freighter, the *Red Delta*. It made an unscheduled stop outside a port in India to pick up the men, and another stop a few miles from Windward to discharge them onto a dory."

"And who is the Mr. L who was going to squeal?" Frank asked.

Bangalore and Nanab both bristled at this. Then Nanab remarked, "Mr. Louis is a friend of Captain Flont's. He owns the dory."

"How did you get the ransom to this country?" Frank asked. "Not by the *Red Delta*, too?"

"Oh, no," Nanab answered. "The ransom rubies were picked up in India, flown by private plane to Europe, and brought to America on an ocean liner which passed in the vicinity of Windward. To avoid customs, small pouches containing the stones were thrown off into Louis's dory by a ship's officer who is one of our group.

"Unfortunately, Louis kept too many of the second shipment for himself. When we exposed him, he threatened to squeal. That is why we are holding him a prisoner here."

"You leased a hunting lodge under the name of Sutter," Frank accused Bangalore, attempting to further prolong the conversation.

Bangalore nodded. "I wanted to impress the prince and make him comfortable. When you boys discovered the place, we left it, telling the prince that this was to avoid the authorities who were after him. He readily agreed to the move."

"You were at the lodge, too?" Joe asked.

"Oh, yes." Bangalore rubbed his hands in pleasure. "I was the one who knocked out your friend Chet Morton. One of the guards attended to you," he said, looking at Frank. "When you found out too much, Nanab quit his job in Washington and came up here to help out."

"Did you turn the krait loose deliberately?" the boy asked.

Bangalore jumped in surprise. "So you saw it? I wish it had bitten you. That snake was a particular pet of mine. I brought it from India. Sometimes it is necessary in matters of this kind to dispose of an enemy without suspicion being directed at the real killer. A krait is an excellent instrument for 'accidental death.' In the excitement of moving from the lodge, the snake got loose, and there was no time for us to search for it."

"You, Nanab, destroyed the letter Mr. Ghapur sent us, but why did you let the falcon be shipped to us?"

Nanab smiled proudly. "I was in charge of sending it. I could have destroyed the bird, too, but Ghapur would have realized I was responsible if you never received it. So I let it go through, then commissioned Ragu to steal it. He failed! He is a fool!"

"You also threw the bomb into our house and stole

the falcon yourself," said Joe. "But who set our boat-house on fire and jammed the *Sleuth*'s gas gauge?"

"I did," Bangalore admitted. "And now that you know the whole story, we will carry out our original plan."

He clapped his hands and several men stepped into the room. In their hands were sturdy rawhide whips!

"You're going to flog us first?" Frank shouted.

An evil smirk on his face, Bangalore said, "We usually plan a quick death with a sleeping potion for our enemies. But because you boys have caused us a great deal of trouble, Nanab and I have decided we will not make it so painless. Before you are put to sleep, we will use these whips and watch you squirm!"

He raised his hand then and cried:

"Flog them!"

CHAPTER XXV

A Touch-and-Go Triumph

Frank and Joe were seized by four guards, while two others raised their whips. But the brothers did not flinch.

Instead, Frank leaned toward Joe. "Here we go again!" he whispered.

A knowing smile crossed Joe's face. The expression was a signal for action. Before the whips could descend, the Hardys, using a jujitsu twist, flung their would-be floggers to the floor, and with the speed of Bengal tigers, tore the whips from the men's hands. The guards shrank back as the boys raised the whips.

Bangalore's jaw dropped. "How did you do that?" he asked, amazed, then added, "I like your courage. My men are skilled in wrestling, but you took them by surprise. It will entertain me to have you demonstrate your skill. Perhaps it can save you a flogging— or maybe even your lives."

Frank and Joe knew that Indians are great lovers

of the sport of wrestling. If the brothers could prolong a match, their father might arrive in time to
rescue them.

"We accept," Frank said. "But let's not decide
our fate on a single fall. That's not sporting. We'll
make it two out of three."

Bangalore laughed raucously. "You are prisoners,
yet you make the terms!"

Nanab spoke up. "Let our men punish them in
the manner they suggest," he said. "We'll teach them
that Indians are the greatest wrestlers."

"Two out of three falls it is!" Bangalore conceded.
"We will go outside," he said, leading the way.

As Frank and Joe laid aside the whips, the smuggler selected two lithe and smooth-muscled guards.
In a crouched position they moved forward quickly,
hands outstretched. But Frank and Joe were ready.
Playing for time, the brothers moved carefully, dart-
ing in, and then leaping back in an effort to catch
their adversaries off balance.

Joe was first to find an opening. Seizing his opponent's left wrist, he spun him around, and pulling
with all his strength, sent the man flying over his
shoulder. The guard landed on his back, groaning as
Joe leaped on him and applied a pinning hold that
in a moment gave Joe his first fall.

Frank's foe cast his eyes on his defeated partner
for a fraction of a second. With the speed of a stooping falcon, Frank charged, catching his adversary in
a leg trip. The man hit the ground hard but jumped

up quickly. Before he recovered, Frank caught him in a headlock that sent both sprawling in the dirt. There was a flurry of dust as the two fought savagely for the advantage.

Suddenly the guard's powerful legs closed about Frank's stomach in a crushing scissors grip. Frank tried in vain to break the tightening hold. As the guard pressed Frank's shoulders nearer and nearer the ground, it appeared that the boy would lose his first fall.

Then the guard shifted his hold slightly to make the pin. Frank, in spite of his weakened condition, saw his advantage and with all his strength he twisted free. Before his surprised opponent could recover, he spun around and seized the guard in a powerful cradle hold and drove him into the ground for a fall.

"Ready for the second fall?" Frank asked, breathing deeply.

The beaten man looked toward Bangalore and jabbered imploringly. The ringleader scowled and replied in their native tongue. Then, while the boys were resting, the Indian leader called forward two more of the guards.

The Hardys were to have new opponents for each fall! They realized it would be senseless, however, to object.

When time was called, they approached their new rivals, and from the start it was apparent that the Hardys had the upper hand through their knowledge of the ancient Japanese art of jujitsu. In the midst of the second fall, a guard ran up, shouting:

"Prince Tava! He is gone! I cannot find him anywhere!"

For a moment everyone froze. Then Bangalore screamed, "This is a trick! And you Hardys are responsible. You must die at once. Nanab, the potion!"

Guards swarmed around Frank and Joe, pinning the boys' arms back, so that they would be unable to resist. Nanab passed one of the poison pellets to his brother. He and Bangalore took up positions before the Hardys, forced their heads back, and pried open their jaws.

With all eyes on the scene, it came as a shock when a voice commanded, "Hands up!"

Fenton Hardy stood at the edge of the clearing. With him were Bhagnav, Ghapur, and Radley and several police officers. As everyone turned, a State Police captain announced:

"You're all under arrest!"

The ringleaders and their guards were quickly seized and handcuffed. Then the officers went to round up the smuggled Indians.

Mr. Hardy ran to his sons. "Are you all right?"

"Yes," Frank assured him. "And we rescued the prince. He's on his way to the hotel."

"Wonderful!" cried Bhagnav and Ghapur.

A search of the premises was instituted at once.

Under the floor boards in Bangalore's bedroom they found the cache of rubies.

"Amazing!" Ghapur commented.

"Enough evidence for a conviction!" Mr. Hardy declared.

After the police left with the prisoners, the Hardys picked up the prince's goshawk and with their friends hurried to Bayport. When they reached the hotel, Prince Tava was in the Hardy suite with Mrs. Hardy and Aunt Gertrude. Hugs, handshakes, and bowing followed with fervor and profusion in the happy reunion. Mr. Delhi and Rahmud Ghapur were particularly pleased to find Prince Tava healthy and unharmed.

After he had recounted his adventures, he pulled his countrymen aside and conversed in their native tongue. Returning shortly, he explained that they were trying to decide on some fitting reward for the Hardys other than the usual fee for services, plus expenses which Mr. Hardy would be paid.

The entire family protested, but Prince Tava turned to Mrs. Hardy and bowed. Then he took off his handsome ruby ring and presented it to her.

"Please accept this token of my deep gratitude," he said with a gentle smile. "I give it to the mother of the two bravest boys I have ever known."

Mrs. Hardy accepted the gift graciously, whereupon the happy group went to dinner in the hotel dining room. Even precise Aunt Gertrude enjoyed the victory celebration immensely.

Early the next morning Chet Morton burst into his friends' room, demanding to hear the whole story. As they finished it, a cablegram was delivered to Frank and Joe.

"Listen to this," Frank cried excitedly. "It's from the Maharajah of Hatavab!" He read aloud:

" 'Cannot thank you enough for aid to Prince Dharmuk. Tava is to continue his schooling. When he returns home next summer will you accompany him and bring the boy who helped you?' "

"That's me!" cried Chet. "Wow, some reward!"

The three boys beamed. "We'll go!" Joe declared. "What a whale of an invitation!"

When the whole group gathered for breakfast, Frank and Joe told their parents about the cablegram. Mr. and Mrs. Hardy heartily approved of their sons accepting the invitation. Silently the boys wondered if the next mystery they would solve would be in India. But long before the following summer arrived, they became involved in THE CLUE IN THE EMBERS.

When the excitement died down, Prince Bhagnav said, "I must explain something to you Hardy boys. I understand my leaving in such a hurry that morning after the bombing gave you cause to wonder about my motives." He laughed. "My trip to New York was to meet another cousin of mine before he could be kidnaped!"

Frank and Joe smiled broadly. After a pause, Mr. Ghapur said:

"I have a gift of my own to offer—the falcon. I want you boys to keep the noble, courageous bird."

Frank and Joe accepted with alacrity, and added, "It would have been pretty hard to part with our hooded hawk."

Suddenly Chet grinned. "Well," he said, "I guess the least I can do is treat you fellows to that dinner I promised. How about all of you coming out to the farm for a big celebration?"

Everyone accepted.

"And bring the falcon with you," Chet urged.

Joe grinned. "We will, if you'll have a pound of raw beef ready for Miss Peregrine as her reward."

Chet readily agreed. "But for all she did, the falcon deserves a sirloin steak!"

"You're right," Frank said. "Without her, we couldn't have solved the mystery."

"Bravo, Miss Peregrine!" Joe said.

And Prince Tava echoed, *"Shabash!* Bravo!"